Yesterdays

Ella Wheeler Wilcox

Contents

YESTERDAYS

BY

Ella Wheeler Wilcox

FOREWORD

This little volume might be called 'Echoes from the land of youthful imaginings'; or 'Ghosts of old dreams.' It has been compiled at the request of Messrs. Gay and Hancock (my only authorised publishers in Great Britain), and contains verses written in my early youth, and which never before (with the exception, perhaps, of three or four) have been placed in book form.

Given the poetical temperament, and a lonely environment, with few distractions, youthful imagination is sure to express itself in mournful wails and despairing moans. Such wails and moans will be found to excess in this little book, and will serve to show better than any amount of common-sense reasoning, how fleeting are the sorrows of youth, and how slight the foundation on which the young build towers of despair.

In the days when these verses were written, each little song represented a few dollars (to my emaciated purse), and so the slightest experience of my own, or of any friend, with every passing mood, every trivial happening, was utilised by my imaginative and thrifty muse.

That the writer has always possessed robust health, and has lived to a good age, is proof positive that the verses are not all expressions of personal experiences, since no human being could have borne such continual agonies and retained life and reason.

All the verses in the book were written while I bore the name of Ella Wheeler, and are quite inconsistent with the ideas and philosophy of

ELLA WHEELER WILCOX.

August 1910.

AN OLD HEART

How young I am! Ah! heaven, this curse of youth
    Doth mock me from my mirror with great eyes,
And pulsing veins repeat the unwelcome truth,
    That I must live, though hope within me dies.

So young, and yet I have had all of life.
    Why, men have lived to see a hundred years,
Who have not known the rapture, joy, and strife
    Of my brief youth, its passion and its tears.

Oh! what are years? A ripe three score and ten
    Hold often less of life, in its best sense,
Than just a twelvemonth lived by other men,
    Whose high-strung souls are ardent and intense.

But having seen all depths and scaled all heights,
    Having a heart love thrilled, and sorrow wrung,
Knowing all pains, all pleasures, all delights,
    Now I would die--but cannot, being young.

Nothing is left me, but supreme despair;
 The bitter dregs that tell of wasted wine.
Come furrowed brow, dull eye, and frosted hair,
 Companions fit for this old heart of mine.

WARP AND WOOF

Through the sunshine, and through the rain
 Of these changing days of mist and splendour,
I see the face of a year-old pain
 Looking at me with a smile half tender.

With a smile half tender, and yet all sad,
 Into each hour of the mild September
It comes, and finding my life grown glad
 Looks down in my eyes, and says 'Remember.'

Says 'Remember,' and points behind
 To days of sorrow, and tear-wet lashes;
When joy lay dead and hope was blind,
 And nothing was left but dust and ashes.

Dust and ashes and vain regret,
 Flames fanned out, and the embers falling.
But the sun of the saddest day must set,
 And hope wakes ever with Springtime's calling.

With Springtime's calling the pulses thrill;

And the heart is tuned to a sweeter measure.
For never a green Spring crossed the hill
    That came not laden with some new pleasure.

Some new pleasure that brings content;
    And the heart looks up with a smile of gladness,
And wonders idly when sorrow went
    Out of the life that seemed all sadness.

That seemed all sadness, and yet grew bright
    With colours we thought could tinge it never.
Yet I think the pain though out of sight,
    Like the warp of the carpet, is there for ever.

There for ever, and by and by
    When the woof wears thin, or draws asunder,
We see the sombre threads that lie
    Intertwining and twisting under.

Twisting under and binding so
    The brighter threads that they may not sever.
Thus the pain of a year ago
    Must stay a part of my life for ever.

SO LONG

The dawn grows red in the eastern sky,
    (Long, so long is the day,)
And I lean from my lattice and sigh and sigh,

As I watch the night fog creeping by
    And vanish over the bay.

The thrush soars up, over green clad hills,
    (The day is long, so long;)
Like liquid silver his music spills,
And ever it quivers, and runs, and trills
    In a glad sweet burst of song.

Under my window there blooms a rose,
    (How long a day can be.)
And I lean and whisper what no soul knows
Of my heart's sorrows and secret woes,
    And the red rose sighs, 'Ah me!'

A ship sails into the waiting bay,
    (The day is long, alack,)
But what would that matter to me, I pray
If the ship that sailed out yesterday
    Should never more come back.

The summer sun rides high and clear,
    (The day is long, so long,)
How long it must be ere it grows to a year--
How deep the sorrow that finds no tear,
    But only a wail of song.

IF I COULD ONLY WEEP

If I could only weep,
I think sweet help with my salt tears would come,
To ease the cruel pain that is so dumb,
        And will not let me sleep.

Down in my heart, down deep
A poisoned arrow burns. It would fall out
And tears would wash the wound, I have no doubt,
        If I could only weep.

Maybe my pulse would leap,
And bring one thrill back, of a vanished day,
Instead of throbbing in this dull, dead way,
        If I could only weep.

O silent Fates who steep
Nectar or gall for us through all the years,
Take what thou wilt, but give me back my tears,
        And let me weep and weep.

WHY SHOULD WE SIGH

Why should we sigh o'er a summer that's dead--
        Let us think of the summer to be.

It always better to look ahead,
For the rose will come again just as red
        And just as fair to see.

Why should we weep o'er a pleasure past--
        Let us look for the pleasure to be.
New shells on the shore by new waves are cast;
Let us prize each new joy more than the last,
        And laugh if the old joy flee.

What folly to die for a love that was--
        Let us live for the one to be.
For time is passing, and will not pause;
How foolish the shore were it sad because
        One wave ebbed out to sea.

Then let us not sing of a year that is fled--
        Though dear its memory be:
For though summer and pleasure and love seem dead,
Love will be sweet, and the rose will be red
        When they blossom for you and me.

A WAKEFUL NIGHT

In the dark and the gloom when winds were fretting
        Like restless children worn out with play,
I said to my heart, 'This task, forgetting--
        Is harder now than it is by day.
For a hungry love that hides from the light,

Like a tiger steals forth, and is bold at night.'

The wind wailed low like a woman weeping;
  Deeper and darker the dense gloom grew.
And, oh! for the old, sweet nights of sleeping,
  When dreams were happy, and love was true.
Before the stars from heaven went out
In a sudden blackness of dread and doubt.

The wind wailed loud, like a madman shrieking,
  And I said to my heart, 'Oh! vain, vain strife;
We cannot forget, and the peace we are seeking
  Can only be won at the end of life.
For see! like a lurid and living spark
The eyes of the tiger shine through the dark.'

The wind sighed low like a sick man dying,
  And the dawn crept silently over the hill.
And I said, 'O heart! there is no use trying,
  We must **remember**, and love on still.'
And the tiger, appeased with its midnight feast,
Fled as the dawn rose red in the East.

IF ONE SHOULD DIVE DEEP

Once more on the beach with the shifting clouds o'er me
  (Like the friends of a day),
And the sea all unchanged, like a true friend before me,
  How the years flow away,

How the summers go by.

The shifting clouds o'er me, the shifting sands under;
    Why need it seem strange,
Why need I feel bitter, and why should I wonder
    That hearts, too, should change
    As the summers go by.

Down here is the path where we wandered together,
    'Neath the midsummer moon.
Her love was sweet as the sweet summer weather,
    And left us as soon,
    And the summers go by.

The bathers laugh loud in the surf over yonder.
    If one should dive deep,
And rise not--no more need he suffer or ponder
    O'er losses, or weep,
    But sink low and sleep
    While the summers go by.

TWO

As I sat in my opera box last night
In a glimmer of gems and a blaze of light,
    And smiling that all might see,
This curious thought came all unsought--
    That there were *two* of me.

One who sat in her silk and lace,
With gems on her bosom and smiles on her face,
    And hot-house blossoms in her hair,
While her fan kept time to the swaying rhyme
    Of the lilting opera air.

And one who sat in the dark somewhere,
With her wan face hid by her falling hair,
    And her hands clasped over her eyes;
And the sickening pain of heart and brain
    Breathed out in long-drawn sighs.

One in the sheen of her opera suit;
And one who was swathed from head to foot,
    In crepe of the blackest dye.
One hiding her heart and playing a part,
    And one with her mask thrown by.

But over the voice of the singer there,
The one who sat with a rose in her hair,
    Seemed ever to hear the moan
Of the one who kept in the dark and wept
    With her desolate heart alone.

NO COMFORT

O mad with mirth are the birds to-day
    That over my head are winging.
There is nothing but glee in the roundelay

That I hear them singing, singing.
On wings of light, up, out of sight--
    I watch them airily flying.
What do they know of the world below,
    And the hopes that are dying, dying?

The roses turn to the sun's warm sky,
    Their sweet lips red and tender;
Oh! life to them is a dream of bliss,
    Of love, and passion, and splendour.
What know they of the world to-day,
    Of hearts that are silently breaking;
Of the human breast, and its great unrest,
    And its pitiless aching, aching?

They send me out into Nature's heart
    For help to bear my sorrow,
Nothing of strength can she impart,
    No peace from her can I borrow.
Her rose-red June and her billing tune,
    Her birds and blossoms only,
Mocked at the grief that seeks relief,
    And leave me lonely--lonely.
If I might stand on the treacherous sand,
    And know I was sinking, sinking,
While the moaning sea sang a dirge for me,--
    Why, that were comfort, I'm thinking.

IT DOES NOT MATTER

It does not matter very much to me
    Through what strange ways my pathway now may lead;
Since I know that it runs away from thee,
    I give it little heed.

It does not matter if in calm or strife,
    There ebb or flow for me the future's tide.
I had but one great longing in my life,
    And that has been denied.

It does not matter if I stand or fall,
    Or walk with kings, or with the rank and file;
Life's loftiest aims and best ambitions all
    Were centred in thy smile.

It does not matter what the world may say:
    I feel no interest in its blame or praise.
I only know we dwell apart to-day,
    And shall through endless days.

It does not matter. For my restless heart
    Is numb to sorrow, or to pleasure's touch.
Since it must be that we two drift apart,
    Why, nothing matters much.

THE UNDER-TONE

In the dull, dim dawn of day I heard
The twitter and thrill of a brown-backed bird,
As he sat and sang in the leafless tree,
A herald of beautiful days to be.

But the minor running under the strain
Went to my heart with a sudden pain,
For never so sad a sound I heard
As the troubled thrill of the brown-backed bird.

Not in the wearisome wash of waves,
With moaning murmur of wrecks and graves,
Not in the weird winds' wildest wail,
Not in the roar of the rushing gale.

Not in the sob of dying years
Are sounds so solemn and full of tears.
O herald of days that are green and glad,
Why was your morning song so sad?

Have you a secret hidden away,
Of sorrow to come with a coming day?
Folded under a folded leaf,
Lies there trouble and bitter grief?

The shadow of death, and tears, and gloom
Coming to me when roses bloom?
Will the beautiful days I long for so
Hold like your song a strain of woe?

What is the secret you hide from me
O herald of days that are to be?
And why was that desolate minor moan
Lurking under your gladdest tone?

WORTH LIVING

I know not what the future may hold,
      Or how to others it seems,
But I know my skies have held more gold
      Than I used to find in my dreams.

Though the whole world sings of hopes death chilled,
      In grateful truth I say,
That my best hopes have been fulfilled,
      And more than fulfilled to-day.

Though oft my arrow I aim at the sun
      To see it fall into the sand,
Yet just as often some work I have done
      Is better than I have planned.

I do not always grasp the pleasure
      For which I reach, maybe;
But quite as frequently over-measure
      Is given by joy to me.

To-morrow may bring a grief behind it

That will thoroughly change my mood;
But we only can speak of a thing as we find it--
　　　And I have found life good.

MORE FORTUNATE

I hold that life more fortunate by far
　　　That sits with its sweet memories alone
　　　And cherishes a joy for ever flown
Beyond the reach of accident to mar.
(Some joy that was extinguished like a star)
　　　Than that which makes the prize so much its own
　　　That its poor commonplacenesses are shown;
(Which in all things, when viewed too closely, are.)

Better to mourn a blossom snatched away
　　　Before it reached perfection, than behold
With dry, unhappy eyes, day after day,
The fresh bloom fade, and the fair leaf decay.
　　　Better to lose the dream, with all its gold,
Than keep it till it changes to dull grey.

HE WILL NOT COME

Take out the blossom in your hair abloom,
  No more it seemeth beautiful, or bright,
And sickening is its subtly sweet perfume--
  He will not come to-night.

Take off the necklace with its sparkling gem,
  And rings that glow and glitter in the light,
And fling them in the case that waits for them--
  He will not come to-night.

Take off the robe a little while ago
  You chose, to make you fairer in his sight;
'Tis ten o'clock. So late you can but know
  He will not come to-night.

He will not come. God grant you strength and grace,
  For never more upon your mortal sight
Shall dawn a glimpse of that beloved face
  That did not come to-night.

He will not come. And through the shadowed years,
  The perfume of that blossom that you wore
Shall stir the fount of salt and bitter tears--
  For one who comes no more.

WORN OUT

I saw a young heart in the grasp of pain;
    With bruised breast, and broken, bleeding wing
Shipwrecked on hopeless love's tempestuous main,
    Lay the poor tortured thing.

It pulsed with all the anguish of despair;
    It ached with all a fond heart's awful power;
Yet I, who stood unhurt above it there,
    Envied its lot that hour.

I, who have wasted all the sacred, deep
    Emotions of my soul in spendthrift fashion,
Until no sorrow now can make me weep--
    No joy stir me with passion.

I, who have scattered here and there the gold
    Of my heart's store, until I spent the whole;
Yet unto each so little gave to hold,
    That I enriched no soul.

I, who have sold the birthright of sweet tears,
    And no more feel a thrill in pulse or brain,
Would gladly have exchanged my tasteless years
    For one salt hour of pain.

Weep on, ye mourners. Glory in the cross
    Of some great grief. Thank God you do not know
The greater grief that comes but with the loss
    Of power to suffer woe.

RONDEAU

As you forgot I may forget,
When summer dews cease to be wet.
　　　When whippoorwills disdain the night,
　　　When sun and moon are no more bright,
And all the stars at midnight set.

When jay birds sing, and thrushes fret,
When snowfalls come in flakes of jet,
　　　When hearts that shelter love are light,
　　　I may forget.

When mortal life no cares beset,
When April brings no violet,
　　　When wrong no longer wars with right,
　　　When all hope's ships shall heave in sight,
And memory holds no least regret,
　　　I may forget.

TRIFLES

Only a spar from a broken ship

Washed in by a careless wave;
But it brought back the smile of a vanished lip,
    And his past peered out of the grave.

Only a leaf that an idle breeze
    Tossed at her passing feet;
But she seemed to stand under the dear old trees,
    And life again was sweet.

Only the bar of a tender strain
    They sang in days gone by;
But the old love woke in her heart again,
    The love they had sworn should die.

Only the breath of a faint perfume
    That floated up from a rose;
But the bolts slid back from a marble tomb,
    And I looked on a dear dead face.

Who vaunts the might of a human will,
    When a perfume or a sound
Can wake a Past that we bade lie still,
    And open a long closed wound?

COURAGE

Whether the way be dark or light
    My soul shall sing as I journey on,
As sweetly sing in the deeps of night

As it sang in the burst of the golden dawn.

Nothing can crush me, or silence me long,
    Though the heart be bowed, yet the soul will rise,
Higher and higher on wings of song,
    Till it swims like the lark in a sea of skies.

Though youth may fade, and love grow cold,
    And friends prove false, and best hopes blight,
Yet the sun will wade in waves of gold,
    And the stars in glory will shine at night.

Though all earth's joys from my life are missed,
    And I of the whole world stand bereft,
Yet dawns will be purple and amethyst,
    And I cannot be sad while the seas are left.

For I am a part of the mighty whole;
    I belong to the system of life and death.
I am under the law of a Great Central,
    And strong with the courage of love and faith.

THE OTHER

All alone with my heart to-night
    I sit, and wonder, and sigh.
What is she like, is she dark, or light,
This other woman who has the right
    To love him better than I?

We never have spoken her name, we two;
          There was no need somehow,
But she lives, and loves, and her heart is true;
From the very first this much I knew,
          So why should it hurt me now.

I fancy her tall, and I think her fair,
          Oh! fairer than I by half.
With sweet, calm eyes, and a wealth of hair,
And a heart as perfectly free from care
          As is her silvery laugh.

She loves rich jewels that flash in the light,
          And revels in costly lace,
And first in the morning, and last at night
She kisses one ring on her finger white;
          (How came those tears on my face?)

She has all best things to make life sweet:
          Youth, and beauty, and gold,
And a love that renders it quite complete.
(I wonder why from my head to my feet
          I feel so deathly cold?)

Yet in all the store of her great delight
          (And she has so much, so much)
She cannot be gladder than I, in the bright
Sweet smile he gave her when he said good night--
          And his warm hand's close, kind touch.

I must put out the light and go to bed;
          I wonder would she care

If she knew, when I knelt with low bowed head,
I prayed for her, but that I said
      His name the last in my prayer?

MAD

Could I but hear you laugh across the street,
Though I, or mine, shared nothing in your glee,
Could I taste that one drop of bitter sweet,
      'Twere more than life to me.

If I might see you coming through the door,
Though with averted face and smileless eye,
Were I allowed that little boon, no more,
      Then I were glad to die.

But oh, my God! this living day on day,
Stripped of the only joy your starved heart had,
Shut in a prison world and forced to stay--
      Why that way souls go mad!

To-day I heard a woman say the earth,
All blossom garlanded, was fair to see.
I laughed with such intensity of mirth,
      The woman shrank from me.

Fair? Why, I see the blackness of the tomb
Where'er I turn, and grave mould on each brow;
And grinning faces peer out of the gloom--

Good God! I *am* mad now.

WHICH

We are both of us sad at heart,
  But I wonder who can say
Which has the harder part,
  Or the bitterer grief to-day.

You grieve for a love that was lost
  Before it had reached its prime;
I sit here and count the cost
  Of a love that has lived its time.

Your blossom was plucked in its May,
  In its dawning beauty and pride;
Mine lived till the August day,
  And reached fruition and died.

You pressed its leaves in a book,
  And you weep sweet tears o'er them.
Dry eyed I sit and look
  On a withered and broken stem.

And now that all is told,
  Which is the sadder, pray,
To give up your dream with its gold,
  Or to see it fade into grey?

LOVE'S BURIAL

See him quake and see him tremble,
    See him gasp for breath.
Nay, dear, he does not dissemble,
    This is really Death.
He is weak, and worn, and wasted,
    Bear him to his bier.
All there is of life he's tasted--
    He has lived a year.

He has passed his day of glory,
    All his blood is cold,
He is wrinkled, thin, and hoary,
    He is very old.
Just a leaf's life in the wild wood,
    Is a love's life, dear.
He has reached his second childhood
    When he's lived a year.

Long ago he lost his reason,
    Lost his trust and faith--
Better far in his first season
    Had he met with death.
Let us have no pomp or splendour,
    No vain pretence here.
As we bury, grave, yet tender,
    Love that's lived a year.

All his strength and all his passion,
    All his pride and truth,
These were wasted, spendthrift fashion,
    In his fiery youth.
Since for him life holds no beauty
    Let us shed no tear,
As we do the last sad duty--
    Love has lived a year.

INCOMPLETE

The summer is just in its grandest prime,
    The earth is green and the skies are blue;
But where is the lilt of the olden time,
When life was a melody set to rhyme,
    And dreams were so real they all seemed true?

There is sun on the meadow, and blooms on the bushes,
    And never a bird but is mad with glee;
But the pulse that bounds, and the blood that rushes,
And the hope that soars, and the joy that gushes,
    Are lost for ever to you and me.

There are dawns of amber and amethyst;
    There are purple mountains, and pale pink seas
That flush to crimson where skies have kist;
But out of life there is something missed--
    Something better than all of these.

We miss the faces we used to know,
  The smiling lips and the eyes of truth.
We miss the beauty and warmth and glow
Of the love that brightened our long ago,
  And ah! we miss our youth.

ON RAINY DAYS

On rainy days old dreams arise,
  From graves where they have lonely lain;
With wan white cheeks and mournful eyes,
  They press against the window pane.
One dream is bolder than the rest:
  She enters at the door and stays,
A welcome yet unbidden guest
  On rainy days.

On rainy days, my dream and I
  Turn back the hands of memory's books:
We sup on pleasures long gone by--
  We drink of unforgotten brooks;
We ransack garrets of the Past,
  We sing old songs, we play old plays;
While hurrying Time looks on aghast,
  On rainy days.

On rainy days, my ghostly dreams
  Come clothed in garments like the mist,
But through that vapoury veiling, gleams

The lustrous eyes my lips have kissed.
A radiant head leans on my heart,
     We walk in well-remembered ways;
But oh! the sorrow when we part,
     On rainy days.

GERALDINE

Just as the sun went bathing in a sea
Of liquid amber, flecked with caps of gold, I told
The sweet old story unto Geraldine, my Queen,
Who long hath made the whole of life for me.

But though she smiled upon me yesterday,
And heaven seemed near because she was so kind, I find
She held me but as one of many men; and then
Dismissed me in her proud, yet gracious way.

Ah, Geraldine! my lady of sweet arts,
There waits for thee not very far away, a day
When thou shalt waken out of tranquil sleep, and weep
Such bitter tears as spring from anguished hearts.

Thou shalt look in thy mirror with dismay
To find upon each feature of thy face, the trace
Of time, the lover who shall follow thee, and see
Thy rare youth slipping suddenly away.

So self-assured, so certain of thy power,

It shall come on thee with a swift surprise. Thine eyes
Appalled, shall fall upon each certain, strange, sad change,
And rob thee of thy triumph in an hour.

And when that day shall come, as come it must,
You then will think of me, sweet Geraldine, my Queen,
And of the faithful heart there tossed away one day,
Before thy dead sea apples turned to dust.

To dust and ashes, leaving nothing more,
That day will come, my lady, I can wait; and Fate
Shall right my wrongs. Thou smilest, Geraldine, my Queen!
Ah well, so have fair women smiled before.

ONLY IN DREAMS

How strange are dreams. Last night I dreamed about you.
    All that old bitterness of loss and pain,
The desolation of my lot without you,
    The keen regret, all, all came back again.

Again I faced that terrible old sorrow;
    Too numb to weep, too cowardly to pray.
Again the blankness of a dread to-morrow
    Filled me with sickly terror and dismay.

I woke in tears; but lo! a moment after,
    When every vestige of my dream was fled,
I broke the silence of my room with laughter,

To think sleep had revived a thing so dead.

Thank God, that only in the realms of fancy
    Can that old sorrow wake again to strife.
No fate is strong enough--no necromancy--
    To make it stir one pulse of my calm life.

My heart is light, my lot is blest without you,
    Our early sorrows are not what they seem,
Now in my slumber, if I dream about you
    I wake to laugh at such an idle dream.

CIRCUMSTANCE

Talk not to me of souls that do conceive
    Sublime ideals, but, deterred by Fate
    And bound by circumstances, sit desolate,
And long for heights they never can achieve.

It is not so. That which we most desire,
    With *understanding*, we at last obtain,
    In part or whole. I hold there is no rain,
No deluge, that can quench a heavenly fire.

Show me thy labour, I straightway will name
    The nature of thy thoughts. Who bends the bow,
    And lets the arrow from the strained string go,
Strikes somewhere near the object of his aim.

We build our ships from timbers of the brain;
  With products of the soul we load the hold;
  Where lies the blame if they bring back no gold,
Or if they spring a leak upon the main?

There is no Fate, no Providence, no Chance,
  The will is all. So be it thou art pure,
  And strong of purpose, thy success is sure;
But fools and sluggards prate of circumstance.

SIMPLE CREEDS

If this were our creed it were creed enough
  To keep us thoughtful and make us brave;
On this sad journey o'er pathways rough
  That lead us steadily on to the grave.

Speak no evil, *and cause no ache*,
Utter no jest that can pain awake;
Guard your actions and bridle your tongue,
Words are adders when hearts are stung.

If this were our aim, it were all, in sooth,
  That any soul needs, to climb to heaven,
And we would not cumber the way of truth
  With dreary dogmas, or rites priest given.

Help whoever, *whenever you can*,

Man for ever needs aid from man.
Let never a day die in the West,
That you have not comforted some sad heart.

Were this our belief we need not brood
      O'er intricate **isms** and modes of faith--
For this embodies the highest goal
      For the life we are living, or after death.

We meet no trials we do not need;
Well borne sorrow is holy seed;
It shall rise in a harvest of golden grain,
And a wise soul ever thanks God for pain.

THE BRIDAL EVE

I stand in the blaze of the candle rays,
      While my merry maidens three
Arrange each tress, and loop my dress,
      And render me fair to see.
But oh! for the eyes that never again
      Will smile like the stars on me.

I sweep down the stair, a bride most fair,
      And some one takes my hand.
I am numb and cold, but the lie is told,
      I smile and my lord is bland.
But oh! for a sight of my rover wild,

Who wanders abroad in the land.

I am queen of the ball and the festal hall;
    I have beauty and youth and gold,
Men bow at the shrine of this lord of mine--
    Lord of his sums untold.
But oh! to be off in the wilds to-night
    With my lover brave and bold.

I dream a dream while the candles gleam,
    While the dancers merrily glide.
Neath the evening star I am speeding far,
    Oh! a good steed do I ride;
And my heart beats high with hope and cheer,
    For my love is at my side.

We ride and sing, and the echoes ring
    With our voices blithe and free,
We have no wealth but our love and health,
    And our cot on the wide green lea;
But I love my love with a mighty love,
    And I know that he loves me.

We ride away in the dying day,
    We ride till we reach the spot
Where all alone in the wilds unknown
    We find our lonely cot.
And I have no wish in the whole wide world,
    And I know that my love has not.

With a dreary moan the viols groan,
    And the dancers pause for breath,
And my lord says, 'Dear, you are ill, I fear,

You are paler than your wreath.'
O God! O God! to be out in the night,
     Riding with love or death.

GOOD NIGHT

The day is at its golden height,
     No shadow falls on sea or land;
And yet to thee I say Good night,
     As we stand here hand clasped in hand,
     Good night--Good night.

The laughing waves are summer blue,
     The bees hum in the sun's warm light;
But frosts of winter chill me through,
     I shiver as I say Good night.
     Good night--Good night.

How often at the close of day
     With smiling lips we've said those words:
And listened as we turned away
     To hear them echoed by the birds,
     Good night--Good night.

We did not dream then of this hour,
     This sad, sad hour for you and me;
We did not dream there was a power
     Could force us for eternity

To say Good night.

Good night--nay, turn your eyes away;
      I cannot bear their tender light.
Now evermore to golden day,
      To golden hope, a last Good night,
      Good night--Good night.

NO PLACE

When days grow long, and brain and hands grow weary,
      And hot the city street,
Forth to the haunts, by cooling winds made cheery
      We fly with willing feet.

We leave our cares and labours all behind us,
      The city's noise and din,
And, hid securely where they cannot find us,
      We drink the sunshine in.

But when the days grow long with bitter sorrow,
      And hearts grow sick with woe,
Where are the haunts that we may seek to-morrow?
      Where can we hide or go?

Holds earth no nook, where hearts with sorrow breaking,
      May find a summer's rest?
A season's respite from the weary aching
      That gnaws within the breast?

O God! if we could fly and leave behind us
    Our crosses and our grief,
Could hide a season where they could not find us,
    What infinite relief.

FOUND

Found--as I rushed through the great world's mart,
    In a race for gold and a pleasure quest,
A passionate, throbbing human heart
    Suddenly found in my breast.

I had always laughed at the foolish word;
    I had said aloud in my boasting glee,
That never a heart in my bosom stirred,
    That my **brain** governed me.

I was proud with the sense of my might and power
    'It is will, not heart that wins,' I said.
But I suddenly found one sad, strange hour
    That the strength of my will had fled.

For up in my breast there rose supreme
    A strong man's heart, and all on fire:
Drunk with the wine of a wild, sweet dream,
    And tortured with desire.

It is tossed with hope, and fear, and doubt,

It is mad with the fever of love's unrest,
I wish to God I could pluck it out--
    This heart I found in my breast.

A MAN'S REVERIE

How cold the old porch seems. A dreary chill
    Creeps upward from the river at twilight,
    And yet, I like to linger here at night,
And dream the summer tarries with us still.

The summer and the summer guests, or guest.
    (Men rarely dream in plurals.) Over there
    Beyond the pillars, stands the rustic chair,
As bare and empty as a robin's nest.

No pretty head reclines its golden bands
    Against the back. No playful winds disclose
    Distracting glimpses of embroidered hose:
No palm leaf waves in dainty, dangerous hands.

How cold it is! That star up yonder gleams
    A white ice sickle from the heavenly eaves.
    That bleak wind from the river sighs and grieves,
Perchance o'er some poor fellow's broken dreams.

Come in, and shut the door, and leave that star
    To watch above the lonely portico.
    Summer and summer guests and dreams must go.

Well, Fate was kind to leave me my cigar.

WHEN MY SWEET LADY SINGS

When she, my lady, smiles,
I feel as one who, lost in darksome wilds,
Sees suddenly the sun in middle sky
Shining upon him like a great glad eye.
     When my sweet lady smiles.

When she, my lady laughs,
I feel as one who some elixir quaffs;
Some nameless nectar, made of wines of suns,
And through my veins a subtle iveresse runs.
     When my sweet lady laughs.

And when my lady talks,
I am as one who by a brooklet walks,
Some sweet-tongued brooklet, which the whole long day,
Holds converse with the birds along the way.
     When my loved lady talks.

And when my lady sings,
Oh then I hear the beat of silver wings;
All that is earthly from beneath me slips,
And in the liquid cadence of her lips
I float, so near the Infinite, I seem
Lost in the glory of a white starred dream.
     When my sweet lady sings.

SPECTRES

How terrible these nights are when alone
          With our scarred hearts, we sit in solitude,
And some old sorrow, to the world unknown,
          Does suddenly with silent steps intrude.

After the guests departed, and the light
          Burned dimly in my room, there came to me,
As noiselessly as shadows of the night,
          The spectre of a woe that used to be.

Out of the gruesome darkness and the gloom
          I saw it peering; and, in still despair,
I watched it gliding swift across the room,
          Until it came and stood beside my chair.

Why, need I tell thee what its shape or name?
          Thou hast thy secret hidden from the light:
And be it sin or sorrow, woe or shame,
          Thou dost not like to meet it in the night.

And yet it comes. As certainly as death,
          And far more cruel since death ends all pain,
On lonesome nights we feel its icy breath,
          And turn and face the thing we fancied slain.

With shrinking hearts, we view the ghastly shape;

We look into its eyes with fear and dread,
And know that we can never more escape
    Until the grave doth fold us with the dead.

On the swift maelstrom of the eddying world
    We hurl our woes, and think they are no more.
But round and round by dizzy billows whirled,
    They reach out sinewy arms and swim to shore.

ONLY A LINE

Only a line in the paper,
    That somebody read aloud,
At a table of languid boarders,
    To the dull indifferent crowd.

Markets and deaths--and a marriage:
    And the reader read them all.
How could he know a hope died then,
    And was wrapped in a funeral pall.

Only a line in the paper,
    Read in a casual way,
But the glow went out of one young life,
    And left it cold and grey.

Colder than bleak December,
    Greyer than walls of rock,
But the reader paused, and the room grew full

Of laughter and idle talk.

If one slipped off to her chamber,
    Why, who could dream or know,
That one brief line in the paper
    Had sent her away with her woe?

Away into lonely sorrow,
    To bitter and blinding tears;
Only a line in the paper,
    But it meant such desolate years.

PARTING

Lean down, and kiss me, O my love, my own;
    The day is near when thy fond heart will miss me;
And o'er my low green bed, with bitter moan,
    Thou wilt lean down, but cannot clasp or kiss me.

How strange it is, that I, so loving thee,
    And knowing we must part, perchance to-morrow,
Do comfort find, thinking how great will be
    Thy lonely desolation, and thy sorrow.

And stranger--sadder, O mine own other part,
    That I should grudge thee some surcease of weeping;
Why do I not rejoice, that in thy heart,
    Sweet love will bloom again when I am sleeping?

Nay, make no promise. I would place no bar
     Upon thy future, even wouldst thou let me.
Thou hast, thou dost, well love me, like a man:
     And, like a man, in time thou wilt forget me.

Why should I care, so near the Infinite--
     Why should I care, that thou wilt cease to miss me?
O God! these earthly ties are knit so tight--
     Quick, quick, lean lower, O my love, and kiss me!

ESTRANGED

So well I knew your habits and your ways,
That like a picture painted on the skies,
At the sweet closing of the summer days,
     You stand before my eyes.

I see you on the old verandah there,
While slow the shadows of the twilight fall,
I see the very carving on the chair
     You tilt against the wall.

The West grows dim. The faithful evening star
Comes out and sheds its tender patient beam.
I almost catch the scent of your cigar,
     As you sit there and dream.

But dream of what? I know your outward life--
Your ways, your habits; know they have not changed.

But has one thought of me survived the strife
    Since we two were estranged?

I know not of the workings of your heart;
And yet I sometimes make myself believe
That I perchance do hold some little part
    Of reveries at eve.

I think you could not wholly put away
The memories of a past that held so much.
As birds fly homeward at the close of day,
    A word, a kiss, a touch,

Must sometimes come and nestle in your breast
And murmur to you of the long ago.
Oh do they stir you with a vague unrest?
    What would I give to know!

BEFORE AND AFTER

Before I lost my love, he said to me:
    'Sweetheart, I like deep azure tints on you.'
But I, perverse as any girl will be
    Who has too many lovers, wore not blue.

He said, 'I love to see my lady's hair
    Coiled low like Clytie's--with no wanton curl.'
But I, like any silly, wilful girl,
    Said, 'Donald likes it high,' and wore it there.

He said, 'I wish, love, when you sing to me,
     You would sing sweet, sad things--they suit your voice.'
I tossed my head, and sung light strains of glee--
     Saying, 'This song, or that, is Harold's choice.'

But now I wear no colour--none but blue.
     Low in my neck I coil my silken hair.
He does not know it, but I strive to do
     Whatever in his eyes would make me fair.

I sing no songs but those he loved the best.
     (Ah! well, no wonder: for the mournful strain
Is but the echo of the voice of pain,
     That sings so mournfully within my breast.)

I would not wear a ribbon or a curl
     For Donald, if he died from my neglect--
Oh me! how many a vain and wilful girl
     Learns true love's worth, but--when her life is wrecked.

AN EMPTY CRIB

Beside a crib that holds a baby's stocking,
A tattered picture book, a broken toy,
A sleeping mother dreams that she is rocking
     Her fair-haired cherub boy.

Upon the cradle's side her light touch keeping,

She gently rocks it, crooning low a song;
And smiles to think her little one is sleeping,
    So peacefully and long.

Step light, breathe low, break not her rapturous dreaming,
Wake not the sleeper from her trance of joy,
For never more save in sweet slumber-seeming
    Will she watch o'er her boy.

God pity her when from her dream Elysian
She wakes to see the empty crib, and weep;
Knowing her joy was but a sleeper's vision,
    Tread lightly--let her sleep.

THE ARRIVAL

'What do I hear at the window?
    Did some one call me?' Nay,
It was only the wind, my darling,
    Grieving the night away.
Only the wind and the casement
    Talking as two friends may.

'But now I hear some one speaking,
    Oh listen and you will hear.'
It is only the night bird calling
    To her mate in sudden fear.
Only the dead leaves falling;
    The last lone leaves of the year.

'But now there is some one coming,
      I hear a step on the stair.'
Nay, nay, it is nothing, darling,
      Rest, and be free from care.
I have just been out in the hallway,
      I am sure there is no one there.

Never a knock at the doorway,
      Never a step in the hall,
Yet the King is coming, coming,--
      How lightly his footsteps fall.
A sigh, and a straightening downward--
      And silence is over all.

GO BACK

When winds of March by the springtime bidden
      Over the great earth race and shout,
Forth from my breast where it long hath hidden
      My same old sorrow comes creeping out.

I think each winter--its life is ended,
      For it makes no stir while the snows lie deep.
I say to myself, 'Its soul has blended
      Into the past where it lay asleep.'

But as soon as the sun, like some fond lover,
      Smiles and kisses the earth's round cheeks,

This sad, sad sorrow throws off its cover,
    And out of the depths of its anguish, speaks.

In every bud by the wayside springing
    It finds a sword for its half-healed wounds;
In every note that the thrush is singing
    It hears the saddest of minor sounds.

In the cup of gold that the sun is spilling
    It finds, unsweetened, a drop of gall;
It sees through the warp that the Spring is filling,
    The black threads twining in under it all.

Go back, O spring! till pain, forsaking
    These haunts of sorrow, shall sink to rest.
Go back! go back! for my heart is breaking,
    And the same old anguish hurts my breast.

WHY I LOVE HER

Why do I love my sweetheart? Well
    I really never tried to tell.
I love her mayhap for her smile,
    So innocent and free from guile.

Perhaps I love her for her mien,
    So calmly cheerful and serene;
Or it may be her silken hair,
    First caught and tangled Cupid there.

And since I came to analyse;
  Her chiefest beauty is her eyes.
Her mouth, too, that is Cupid's bow--
  Perhaps that's why I love her so.

And now I think of it, her voice
  First made my rusty heart rejoice
And then her hand--'tis my belief
  It quite outvies the lily leaf.

Perhaps I love her for her ways
  That blend in with the sunny days.
Tush--to be brief and plain with you,
  I love her *just because I do*.

DISCONTENT

Like a thorn in the flesh, like a fly in the mesh,
  Like a boat that is chained to shore,
The wild unrest of the heart in my breast
  Tortures me more and more.
I wot not why, it should wail and cry
  Like a child that is lost at night,
For it knew no grief, but has found relief,
  And it is not touched with blight.

It has had of pleasure full many a measure;
  It has thrilled with love's red wine;

It has hope and health, and youth's rare wealth--
    Oh rich is this heart of mine.
Yet it is not glad--it is wild and mad
    Like a billow before it breaks;
And its ceaseless pain is worse than vain,
    Since it knows not why it aches.

It longs to be, like the waves of the sea
    That rise in their might and beat
And dash and lunge, and hurry and plunge,
    And die at the grey rocks' feet.
It wearies of life and it sickens of strife
    And yet it tires of rest.
Oh! I know not why it should ache and cry--
    'Tis a troublesome heart at best.

Though not understood, I think it a good
    And God-like discontent.
It springs from the soul that longs for its goal--
    For the source from which it was sent.
Then surge, O breast, with thy wild unrest--
    Cry, heart, like a child at night,
Till the mystic shore of the Evermore
    Shall dawn on thy eager sight.

A DREAM

In the night I dreamed that you had died,
    And I thought you lay in your winding sheet;

And I kneeled low by your coffin side,
  With my cheek on your heart that had ceased to beat.

And I thought as I looked on your form so still,
  A terrible woe, and an awful pain,
Fierce as vultures that slay and kill,
  Tore at my bosom and maddened my brain.

And then it seemed that the chill of death
  Over me there like a mantle fell,
And I knew by my fluttering, failing breath
  That the end was near, and all was well.

I woke from my dream in the black midnight--
  It was only a dream at worst or best--
But I lay and thought till the dawn of light,
  Had the dream been true we had both been blest.

Better to kneel by your still dead form,
  With my cheek on your breast, and die that way,
Than to live and battle with night and storm,
  And drift away from you day by day.

Better the anguish of death and loss,
  The sharp, quick pain, and the darkness, then,
Than living on with this heavy cross
  To bear about in the world of men.

THE NIGHT

Oh! give me the night, the dark, dark night,
    The night with never a star.
When the stars are veiled and the moon has sailed
    Beyond the horizon's bar.
When thought grows weary of groping its way
    Through darkness dense and deep,
And buries its head in oblivion's bed,
    Wrapped warm in the mantle of sleep.

For I hate the night, the moon-white night,
    The night with a pallid face,
When a million eyes from the watchful skies
    Peers into each secret place.
For thought awakes and the old wound aches,
    And Sorrow she cannot rest,
But all night long walks to and fro
    Through the aisles of my troubled breast.

And Memory thinks it her royal hour
    When the heavens glitter and shine;
And she fills the cup of the past well up
    With a bitter and scalding wine.
And she calls for a toast to the ghastly ghost
    Of a joy that used to be.
And that terrible face in the dear old moon
    Stares steadily down at me.
So give me the night, the deep, dark night,
    The night with never a star,
When the skies are veiled and the moon has sailed

Beyond the horizon's bar.

NEW YEAR

The year like a ship in the distance
    Comes over life's mystical sea.
We know not what change of existence
    'Tis bringing to you or to me.
But we wave out the ship that is leaving
    And we welcome the ship coming in,
Although it be loaded with grieving,
    With trouble, or losses, or sin.

Old year passing over the border,--
    And fading away from our view;
All idleness, sloth, and disorder,
    All hatred and spite go with you.
All bitterness, gloom, and repining
    Down into your stronghold are cast.
Sail out where the sunsets are shining,
    Sail out with them into the past.

Good reigns over all; and above us,
    As sure as the sun gives us light,
Great forces watch over and love us,
    And lead us along through the night.
Look up, and reach out, and believe them--
    Believe in your infinite worth.
Do nothing to wound or to grieve them,

And you shall find heaven on earth.

The body needs conflict and tussle,
    To render it forceful and grand;
The soul, too, has sinew and muscle,
    Which sorrow alone can expand.
Though troubles come faster and faster,
    Rise up, brace yourself for each blow;
It is only Fate's great fencing Master
    Instructing your spirit to grow.

The new ship comes nearer and nearer,
    We know not what freight she may hold;
Hope stands at the helm there to steer her,
    Our hearts are courageous and bold.
Sail in with new joys and new sorrows,
    Sail in with new banners unfurled,
Sail in with unwritten to-morrows,
    Sail in with new tasks for the world.

REVERIE

The day has been wild and stormy,
    And full of the wind's unrest,
And I sat down alone by the window,
    While the sunset dyed the West;
And the holy rush of twilight,
    As the day went over the hill,
Like the voice of a spirit seemed speaking

And saying, 'Peace be still.'

Then I thought with sudden longing,
    That it might be so with my woes;
That the life so wild and restless,
    When it reached the eve's repose,
Might glow with a sudden glory,
    And be crowned with peace and rest;
And the holy calm of twilight
    Might come to my troubled breast.

All of the pain and passion
    That trouble my life's long day
As the winds go down at sunset,
    May suddenly pass away.
And the wild and turbulent billows,
    That surge in my heart at will,
Shall be hushed into calm and silence
    By the whisper, 'Peace be still.'
And my soul grew full of patience,
    And I said, 'I can bear it all,
Though the day be long and stormy,
    The twilight at last must fall.'

THE LAW

The tide of love swells in me with such force,
    It sweeps away all hate and all distrust.
As eddying straws and particles of dust

Are lost by some swift river in its course.

So much I love my friends, my life, my art,
    Each shadow flies; the light dispels the gloom.
Love is so fair, I find I have no room
    For anything less worthy in my heart.

Love is a germ which we can cultivate--
    To grace and perfume sweeter than the rose,
Or leave neglected while our heart soil grows
    Rank with that vile and poison thistle, hate.

Love is a joyous thrush, that one can teach
    To sing sweet lute-like songs which all may hear.
Or we can silence him and tune the ear
    To caw of crows, or to the vulture's screech.

Love is a feast; and if the guests divide
    With all who pass, though thousands swell the van,
There shall be food and drink for every man;
    The loaves and fishes will be multiplied.

Love is the guide. I look to heights above
    So beautiful, so very far away;
Yet I shall tread their sunlit peaks some day,
    Since close in mine I hold the hand of love.

Love is the law. But yield to its control
    And thou shalt find all things work for the best,
And in the calm, still heaven of thy breast,
    That God, Himself, sits talking with thy soul.

SPIRIT OF A GREAT CONTROL

Spirit of a Great Control,
    Gird me with thy strength and might,
Essence of the Over-Soul--
    Fill me, thrill me with thy light;
Though the waves of sorrow beat
    Madly at my very feet,
Though the night and storm are near,
    Teach me that I need not fear.

Though the clouds obscure the sky,
    When the tempest sweeps the lands,
Still about, below, on high,
    God's great solar system stands.
Never yet a star went out.
    What have I to fear or doubt?--
I, a part of this great whole,
    Governed by the Over-Soul.

Like the great eternal hills,
    Like the rock that fronts the wave,
Let me meet all earthly ills
    With a fearless heart and brave;
Like the earth that drinks the rain,
    Let me welcome floods of pain,
Till I grow in strength to be
    Worthy of my source in Thee.

NOON

As some contented bird doth coo
  She trilled a song of fond delight,
  The while she spread the cloth of white,
And set the cups and plates for two.

She leaned beyond the window sill,
  And looked along the busy street,
  And listened for his coming feet.
The skies were calm, the winds were still.

'O love, my love, why art thou late?
  The kettle boils, the cloth is spread,
  The clock points close to noon,' she said.
O clock of time! O clock of fate!

She heard the moon's glad sound of cheer;
  (The hiss, the whirl, the crash, the creak,
  Of maddened wheels, the awful shriek
Of awestruck men--she did not hear.)

She lightly tripped about the room,
  And near the window, where his eyes
  Might greet it with a pleased surprise,
She placed a pot of fragrant bloom.

Strange nervous steps were at the gate.
  Why grew her heart so cold, so numb?
  The clock struck twelve, the noon had come.

Ah! noon of time! O noon of fate!

A shattered vase beside the wall;
        A young face grey with awful fear,
        A rigid shape, a covered bier,
A shadowed life, and that is all.

THE SEARCH

The rain falls long, and the rain falls light,
        With a desolate drip--drop, sad to hear.
But never a star shines through the night
        As I sit afar, from the world anear.

Down in the parlour some one sings;
        The children laugh in the nursery hall;
But my heart like a bird has spread its wings,
        And leaves the music, and mirth, and all.

Out in the rain and the eerie night,
        Into the darkness it speeds away.
Ah me! ah me! 'tis a gruesome flight,
        Seeking for you till the dawn of day.

If it only knew which way to go;
        Where you wander, or where you lie.
To valleys of sunshine, or hills of snow,
        Thither at once my heart would fly.

Fly and follow wherever you led,
    Over the desert and over the wave;
Or if it found you lying dead,
    It would sit in the rain by your lonely grave.

Sit in the rain, and cover the grass
    With passionate kisses above your face.
Sit there waiting till death should pass,
    And bear it to you in his strong embrace.

But hither and thither all is vain,
    It flies in the darkness, and seeks for you.
Back in the morning, drenched with rain,
    The poor thing cometh with never a clue.

But all night long the rain falls down,
    Like a poor crazed thing that has lost its way,
Through the forest and through the town
    It searches for you till the break of day.

A MAN'S GOOD-BYE

Do you think, dear, as you say
Such a light good-bye to-day,
That this parting time may be
Mayhaps less to you, than me?

What a wonder of surprise
Looks out from your sunny eyes.

'Just a nice acquaintance.' So
We have called it, dear, I know.

Now you end it with a word,
While my inmost soul is stirred.
No--you cannot understand.
But, dear, as I touch your hand,

Listening to your light good-bye,
All a man's roused passions cry
Like a tiger, stirred, at bay.
Oh! you draw your hand away.

'I've no right to speak so?' Pray
Was it **your** right day by day
By your sweet coquettish arts
To invade my heart of hearts?

It is death to let you go.
You will hate me, dear, I know;
But I swear, ere you go hence,
I will have some recompense.

For those fires you lit in vain,
Cheeks and lips shall bear the stain
Of my kisses till you die.
Go now! this is my good-bye.

AT THE HOP

'Tis time to dress. Dost hear the music surging
       Like sobbing waves that roll up from the sea?
Yes, yes, I hear--I yield--no need of urging;
       I know your wishes,--send Lisette to me.

I hate the ballroom; hate its gilded pleasure;
       I hate the crowd within it, well you know;
But what of that? I am your lawful treasure--
       And when you would display me I must go.

You bought me with a mother's pain and trouble.
       I've been a great expense to you alway.
And now, if you can sell me, and get double
       The sum I cost--why, what have I to say?

You've done your duty: kept me in the fashion,
       And shown me off at every stylish place.
'Twas not your fault I had a heart of passion;
       'Twas not your fault I ever *saw* his face.

The dream was brief, and beautiful, and tender,
       (O God! to live those golden hours once more.
The silver moonlight, and his dark eyes' splendour,
       The sky above us, and the sea before.)

Come, come, Lisette, bring out those royal laces;
       To-night must make the victory complete.
Among the crowd of masked and smiling faces,

I'll move with laughter, and with smiles most sweet.

Make me most fair! with youth and grace and beauty,
     I needs must conquer bloated age and gold.
She shall not say I have not done my duty;
     I'm ready now--a daughter to be sold!

MET

How odd and strange seems our meeting
     Like a grim rendezvous of the dead.
All day I have sat here repeating
     The commonplace things that we said.
They sounded so oddly when uttered--
     They sound just as odd to me now;
Was it we, or our two ghosts who muttered
     Last evening, with simper and bow?

I had grown used to living without you.
     In revel and concert and ball,
I had flown from much thinking about you,
     And your picture I turned to the wall.
For to call back the dream that was broken,
     To fancy your hand on my hair,
To remember the words we had spoken,
     Was madness, and gall, and despair.

I knew I could never forget you;
     But I wanted to put you away.

And now, just to think how I met you--
>It has seemed like a nightmare all day.
We two with our record of passion,
>We two who have been as one heart,
To meet in that calm, quiet fashion,
>And chat for a moment and part.

We two who remember such blisses
>Not heaven itself can eclipse,
We two who had kissed with the kisses
>That draw out the soul through the lips,
We two who have known the ideal,
>The rare perfect love in its might--
Nay, nay, they were ghosts, and not real,
>Who met, and who parted, last night.
They were ghosts, unprepared for the meeting;
>'Twas a chance rendezvous of the dead;
And all day I sit here repeating
>The odd sounding words that were said.

RETURNED BIRDS

My heart to-day is like a southern wood,
>Through summer months it has been drunk with heat;
>And slumbered on unmindful of the beat
Of life beyond it: sleep alone seemed good.

Now milder Autumn's tints are in the sky;
>The fervid heats of summer noons depart;

And backward to the old haunts in my heart
The golden robins and the blue birds fly.

I hear the flutter of their airy wings,
They flock about the Spring's deserted nest,
And suddenly I feel within my breast
The stirring of sweet half-forgotten things.

Bright sunny mornings--golden growing hours--
The building of glad birds among the trees;
Wide open windows and the kindly breeze
Bringing the perfume of half-open flowers.

A blithe face at the window fair with truth;
A mellow laugh that falls like silver spray;
Down through the sunlight of the perfect day,
Ecstatic hopes, that bud with Spring and Youth.

The morning time grew rank with summer blight;
The birds flew northward, fresher fields to find;
And in our hearts we closed the folding blind,
While drooping blossoms withered in the light.

The fair face at the window could not stay;
The laugh grew weary, with a minor strain
That borders on the foreign realm of pain,
And hopes that blossomed, ripened to decay.

Come, happy birds, and sing of vanished joy,
Of that sweet Spring for ever passed away;
No winter lies between us and that day.
(But what is sadder than the sweets that cloy.)

My heart is green with leafage; come and wake
    The old-time echoes with the songs of glee,
    For only echoes now are left to me,
Though bloom and beauty cling to bush and brake.

A CRUSHED LEAF

An hour ago when the wind blew high
    At my lady's window a red leaf beat.
Then dropped at her door, where, passing by,
    She carelessly trod it under her feet.

I have taken it out of the dust and dirt,
    With a tender pity but half defined.
Ah! poor bruised leaf, with your stain and hurt,
    'A fellow-feeling doth make us kind.'

On winds of passion my heart was blown,
    Like an autumn leaf one hapless day.
At my lady's window with tap and moan
    It burned and fluttered its life away.

Bright with the blood of its wasting tide
    It glowed in the sun of her laughing eyes.
What cared she though a stray heart died--
    What to her were its sobs and sighs.

The winds of passion were spent at last,
    And my heart like the leaf in her pathway lay;

And under her slender foot as she passed,
    My lady she trod it and went her way.

So I picked the leaf from its dusty place,
    With a tender pity--too well defined.
And I laid it here in this velvet case,
    Ah! a fellow-feeling doth make us kind.

A CURIOUS STORY

I heard such a curious story
    Of Santa Claus: once, so they say,
He set out to see what people were kind,
    Before he took presents their way.
'This year I will give but to givers,
    To those who make presents themselves,'
With a nod of his head old Santa Claus said
    To his band of bright officer-elves.

'Go into the homes of the happy
    Where pleasure stands page at the door.
Watch well how they live, and report what they give
    To the hordes of God's suffering poor.
Keep track of each cent and each moment;
    Yes, tell me each word, too, they use:
To silver line clouds for earth's suffering crowds,
    And tell me, too, when they refuse.'

So into our homes flew the fairies,

Though never a soul of us knew,
And with pencil and book they sat by and took
        Each action, if false, or if true.
White marks for the deeds done for others--
        Black marks for the deeds done for self.
And nobody hid what he said or he did,
        For no one, of course, sees an elf.

Well, Christmas came all in its season,
        And Santa Claus, so I am told,
With a very light pack of small gifts on his back,
        And his reindeers all left in the fold,
Set out on a leisurely journey,
        And finished ere midnight, they say.
And there never had been such surprise and chagrin
        Before on the breaking of day,

As there was on that bright Christmas morning
        When stockings, and cupboards, and shelves
Were ransacked and sought in, for gifts that were not in--
        But wasn't it fun for the elves!
And what did *I* get? You confuse me--
        I got not one thing, and that's true;
But had I suspected my actions detected
        I would have had gifts, wouldn't you?

JENNY LIND

There was a something in your song, men say

No later singer voices: some strange power
Like to the essence in a rare June day,
    Or like the subtle perfume of a flower.
Awed and inspired, your listeners turned away,
    Baptized in your sweet music's holy shower.
For through that music shone the glorious dower
    Of your great soul: here all the secret lay.

Not for the honours of this earth you sang--
    Not for its gold or glory, not for art,
Not for the fortunes at your fair feet hurled.
    The love of God through all your measures rang,
And each pure note bespoke a noble heart.
    When worth weds genius, lo! they rule the world.

LIFE'S KEY

The hand that fashioned me, tuned my ear
    To chord with the major key,
In the darkest moments of life I hear
Strains of courage, and hope, and cheer
    From choirs that I cannot see.
And the music of life seems so inspired
That it will not let me grow sad or tired.

Yet through and under the major strain,
    I hear with the passing of years,
The mournful minor measure of pain,
Of souls that struggle and toil in vain

For a goal that never nears.
And the sorrowful cadence of good gone wrong,
Breaks more and more into earth's glad song.

And oft in the dark of the night I wake
      And think of sorrowing lives,
And I long to comfort the hearts that ache,
To sweeten the cup that is bitter to take,
      And to strengthen each soul that strives.
I long to cry to them 'Do not fear,
Help is coming and aid is near.'

However desolate, weird, or strange
      Life's melody sounds to you,
Before to-morrow the air may change,
And the Great Director of music arrange
      A programme perfectly new.
And the dirge in minor may suddenly be
Turned into a jubilant song of glee.

BRIDGE OF PRAYER

The bridge of prayer from heavenly heights suspended
      Unites the earth with spirit-realms in Space.
The interests of those separate worlds are blended
      For those whose feet turn often toward that place.

In troubled nights of sorrow and repining,
      When joy and hope seem sunk in dark despair,

We still may see above the shadows shining,
    The gleaming archway of the bridge of prayer.

From that fair height, our souls may lean and listen
    To sounds of music from the farther shore,
And through the vapours, sometimes dear eyes glisten
    Of loved ones who have hastened on before.

And angels come from their Celestial City--
    And meet us half way on the bridge of prayer.
God sends them forth, full of divinest pity
    To strengthen us for burdens we must bear.

Oh! you whose feet walk in some shadowed by-way,
    Far from the scenes of pleasure and delight,
Still free to you hangs this suspended highway,
    Where heavenly glories dawn upon the sight.

And common paths glow with a grace supernal,
    And happiness walks hand in hand with care,
And faith becomes a knowledge fixed, eternal,
    For those who often seek the bridge of prayer.

NEW YEAR

Know this! there is nothing can harm you
    If you are at peace with your soul.
Know this, and the knowledge shall arm you
    With courage and strength to the goal.

Your spirit shall break every fetter,
  And love shall cast out every fear.
And grander, and gladder, and better
  Shall be every added new year.

DECEITFUL CALM

The winds are still; the sea lies all untroubled
  Beneath a cloudless sky; the morn is bright,
Yet, Lord, I feel my need of Thee is doubled;
  Come nearer to me in this blaze of light;
The night must fall,--the storm will burst at length.
  Oh! give me strength.

So well, so well, I know the treacherous seeming
  Of days like this; they are too heavenly fair.
Those waves that laugh like happy children dreaming,
  Are mighty forces brewing some despair
For thoughtless hearts, and ere the hour of need,
  Let mine take heed.

Joy cannot last; it must give place to sorrow
  As certainly as solar systems roll.
I would not wait till that time comes to borrow
  The strength prayer offers to a suffering soul.
Here in the sunlight--yet undimmed by shade,
  I cry for aid.

I dare not lightly drain the cup of pleasure,

Though Thine the hand that proffers me the draught.
Such bitter lees lie lower in the measure,
    I shall need courage, ere the potion's quaffed;
Then strengthen me before that time befall,
    To drink the gall.

I need Thee in my joys and my successes,
    To make me humble, grateful, and not vain.
I need Thee when the weight of sorrow presses
    The tortured heart that cries aloud in pain,
So close great pleasures and great anguish lie.
    Lord, Lord, come nigh.

UN RENCONTRE

Now ought we to laugh or to weep--
    Was it comical, or was it grave?
When we who had waded breast deep
    In passion's most turbulent wave
Met out on an isle in Time's ocean,
With never one thrill of emotion.

We had parted in sorrow and tears;
    Our letters were frequent and wet;
We wrote about pitiless years,
    And we swore we could never forget.
An angel you called me alway,
And I thought you a god gone astray.

We met in an everyday style;
  Unmoved by a tremor or start;
Shook hands, smiled a commonplace smile;
  (With a happy new love in each heart),
And I thought you the homeliest man
As you awkwardly picked up my fan!

And I know (or I haven't a doubt)
  Though you did not say so to my face,
That you thought I was growing too stout:
  I, once your ideal of grace.
And ere the encounter was o'er
Each voted the other a bore.

What a proof that fond passion can die,
  In this prosaic meeting we had!
Now, ought we to laugh or to cry--
  Was it sorrowful, or was it sad?
'Tis a puzzle not worthy our time,
So let's give it up--with this rhyme.

BURNED OUT

Blow out the light: there is no oil to feed it:
  That dim blue light unworthy of the name.
Better to sit with folded hands, I say,
And wait for night to pass, and bring the day,
  Than to depend upon that flickering flame.

Take back your vow: there is no love to bind it:
     Take back this little shining, golden thing.
Better to walk on bravely all alone,
Than strive to hold up, or retain our own,
     By soulless pledge, or fetter of a ring.

When first the lamp was lit, too high you turned it;
     The oil was wasted in a blinding blaze.
Your passion was too ardent in the start--
Set by the lamp: farewell. God gird the heart
     Through darkened hours, and lone and loveless ways.

ONLY A GLOVE

Only a glove that has touched her fingers,
     But it seems to me something half divine.
A delicate fragrance about it lingers,
     And it stirs my blood like wine--
     Yes, thrills and warms me like wine.

So well I remember the night she wore it--
     How I held the hand in its dainty glove,
And whispered sweetly as I leaned o'er it--
     Whispered a tale of love--
     A story of my mad love.

There was mirth, and music, and light and laughter,
     The viols played and the dancers whirled.
We were part of it all--but a moment after

Were alone in love's fair world--
Alone in God's own world.

But now of that night of glow and splendour,
        Of happy hope and beautiful love,
Of youthful dreams that were sweetly tender,
        There is nothing left but a glove,
        Nothing but this one glove.

REMINDERS

When in the early dawn I hear the thrushes,
        And like a flood of waters o'er my heart
The memory of another summer rushes,
        How can I rise up, and perform my part?

When in the languid eve I hear the wailing
        Of the uncomforted sad mourning dove,
Whose grief, like mine, seems deep as unavailing,
        What will I do with all this wealth of love?

When the sweet rain falls over hills and meadows,
        And the tall poplar's silver leaves are wet,
And, like my soul, the world seems draped in shadow,
        How shall I hush this passionate regret?

When the wild bee is wooing the red clover,
        And the fair rose smiles on the butterfly,
Missing thy smile and kiss, O love, my lover,

Who on God's earth so desolate as I?

My tortured senses new despair will borrow
    From those reminders of a vanished day,
That was as full of joy as this of sorrow--
    O beautiful, sad summer keep away!

A DIRGE

Death and a dirge at midnight;
    Yet never a soul in the house
Heard anything more than the throb and beat
    Of a beautiful waltz of Strauss.

Dead, dead, dead, and staring,
    With a ghastly smile on its face;
But the world saw only laughing eyes
    And roses, and billows of lace.

Floating and whirling together,
    Into the beautiful night,
How little you dreamed of the ghastly thing
    I was hiding away from your sight.

Meeting your dark eyes' splendour,
    Feeling your warm, sweet breath,
How could you know that my passionate heart
    Had died a horrible death?

Died in its fever and fervour,
          Died in its beautiful bloom;
And that waltz of Strauss was a funeral dirge,
          Leading the way to the tomb.

But you held my hand at parting,
          And I smiled back a gay good night;
And you never knew of the ghastly corpse
          I was hiding away from your sight.

Yet whenever I hear the Danube--
          Under its pulsing strain,
I catch the wail of the funeral dirge,
          And my heart dies over again.

NOT ANCHORED

My heart is like a ship that finds no rest,
Tossed here and there upon the stormy breast
Of loves of many hearts too oft conferred.

Thy love is like the harbour, safe and still,
Into whose calm that ship may glide at will,
Under the slope of God's Eternal Will.

So near the perfect peace that knows no word;
Yet with an empty, white emotion stirred,
It folds its wings like some contented bird.

At rest, and yet not **anchored**; and some day
Out of the restful peace of this calm bay
The winds of Fate will drift it far away.

THE NEW LOVE

I thought my heart was death chilled,
     I thought its fires were cold;
But the new love, the new love,
     It warmeth like the old.

I thought its rooms were shadowed
     With the gloom of endless night;
But the new love, the new love,
     It fills them full of light.

I thought the chambers empty,
     And proclaimed it unto men;
But the new love, the new love,
     It peoples them again.

I thought its halls were silent,
     And hushed the whole day long;
But the new love, the new love,
     It fills them full of song.

Then here is to the new love,
     Let who will sing the old;
The new love, the new love,

'Tis more than fame or gold.

For it gives us joy for sorrow,
    And it gives us warmth for cold;
Oh! the new love, the new love,
    'Tis better than the old.

AN EAST WIND

The glitter of wheels far down the street
    (Ah me, and alack a day.)
And I heard the thud of his horse's feet
    Beating a roundelay.
And I felt a little song coming, coming
Over my lips as humming, humming,
    I turned my eyes that way.

Somebody passed, who was wont to pause:
    (Ah me, and alack a day.)
He bowed and smiled; yet for some cause
    The mirth went out of my lay.
A wind from the east rose, sighing, sighing,
I felt my little song dying, dying,
    She laughed as they rode away.

CHEATING TIME

Kiss me, sweetheart. One by one
Swift and sure the moments run.

Soon, too soon, for you and me
Gone for aye the day will be.

Do not let time cheat us then,
Kiss me often and again.

Every time a moment slips
Let us count it on our lips

While we're kissing, strife and pain
Cannot come between us twain.

If we pause too long a space,
Who can tell what may take place?

You may pout, and I may scold,
Souls be sundered, hearts grow cold;

Death may come, and love take wings;
Oh! a thousand cruel things

May creep in to spoil the day,
If we throw the time away.

Let us time, the cheater, cheat,
Kiss me, darling, kiss me, sweet.

ONLY A SLIGHT FLIRTATION

'Twas just a slight flirtation,
  And where's the harm, I pray,
In that amusing pastime
  So much in vogue to-day?

Her hand was plighted elsewhere
  To one she held most dear,
But why should she sit lonely
  When other men were near?

They walked to church together,
  They sat upon the shore.
She found him entertaining,
  He found her something more.

They rambled in the moonlight;
  It made her look so fair.
She let him praise her beauty,
  And kiss her flowing hair.

'Twas just a nice flirtation.
  'So sad the fellow died.
Was drowned one day while boating,
  The week she was a bride.'

A life went out in darkness,

A mother's fond heart broke,
A maiden pined in secret--
    With grief she never spoke.

While robed in bridal whiteness,
    Queen of a festal throng,
She moved, whose slight flirtation
    Had wrought this triple wrong.

WHAT THE RAIN SAW

Winds of the summer time what are you saying,
    What are ye seeking, and what do you miss?
Locks like the thistledown floating and straying,
    Cheeks like the budding rose, tinted to kiss.

See ye yon mist rising up from the river?
    That is the spirit of yesterday's rain.
Go to it, fly to it, call to it, cry to it,
    What did ye see when ye fell on the plain?

Rosewood, and velvet, and pansies, and roses,
    Blossoms from loving hands tenderly cast.
Lids like the leaves of a lily that closes
    After its brief little day-life is past.

Beautiful hands on a beautiful bosom,
    Folded so quietly, folded in rest.
Mouth like the bud of a white-petalled blossom,

Creased where the lips of an angel had pressed.

Lower, and lower, and lower, and lower,
    Dust unto dust--but a mound on the plain.
Left alone, lonely, this, and this only,
    Saw we, and see we to-day, said the rain.

Winds of the summer time vain is your seeking,
    Vain is your calling with sobs in your breath.
Lips that are tender, eyes full of splendour,
    Wooed away, sued away, vanished with death.

AFTER

After the end that is drawing near
    Comes, and I no more see your face
Worn with suffering, lying here,
    What shall I do with the empty place?

You are so weary, that if I could
    I would not hinder, I would not keep
The great Creator of all things good,
    From giving his own beloved sleep.

But over and over I turn this thought.
    After they bear you away to the tomb,
And banish the glasses, and move the cot,
    What shall I do with the empty room?

And when you are lying at rest, my own,
  Hidden away in the grass and flowers,
And I listen in vain for your sigh and moan,
  What shall I do with the silent hours?

O God! O God! in the great To Be
  What canst Thou give me to compensate
For the terrible silence, the vacancy,
  Grim, and awful, and desolate?

Passing away, my beautiful one,
  Out of the old life into the new.
But when it is over, and all is done,
  God of the Merciful, what shall I do?

Sweetest of slumber, and soundest rest,
  No more sorrow, and no more gloom.
I am quite contented, and all is best,--
  But the empty bed--and the silent room!

OUR PETTY CARES

Our petty cares wear on us so,--
More cruel than our great despairs,
More rasping than a mighty woe,
  Our petty cares.

Less need of strength hath he who bears
Courageously some stinging blow,

Of Fate which takes him unawares.

Not solitary griefs we know
Induce old age and whitening hairs;
But that malicious, endless row--
          Our petty cares.

THE SHIP AND THE BOAT

In the great ship Life we speed along,
          With sails and pennons spread.
And tethered, beside the great ship, glide
          The mystic boats for the dead.

Over the deck of the ship of Life
          Our loved and lost we lower.
And calm and steady, his small boat ready,
          Death silently sits at the oar.

He rows our dead away from our sight--
          Away from our hearing or ken.
We call and cry for a last good-bye,
          But they never come back again.

The ship of Life bounds on and on;
          The river of Time runs fast;
And yet more swift our dear dead drift
          For ever back into the Past.

We do not forget those loved and lost,
      But they fade away like a dream:
As we hurry along on the current strong
      Of Time's great turbulent stream.

On and on, and ever away,
      Our sails are filled by the wind;
We see new places, we meet new faces,
      And the dead are far behind.

Their boats have drifted into the sea
      That laves God's holy feet.
But the river's course, too, seeks that source,
      So the ship and the boat shall meet.

COME NEAR

Come near to me, I need Thy glorious presence.
      Through the dense darkness of this troubled hour
Shine on my soul, and fill it with the essence
      Of Thy pervading and uplifting power.
      Come near, come near to me!

Come nearer yet, I have no strength to reach Thee;
      My soul is like a bird with broken wings.
Lean down from Thy fair height of peace, and teach me
      The balm Thy touch to mortal bruises brings.
      Lean down, O God, lean down!

Come near, and yet if those eternal places
   Hold greater tasks to occupy Thy hands,
Send Thy blest angels whose celestial faces
   Smile sometimes on us from the spirit lands.
   Send one, send one to me!

I must have help. I am so weak and broken
   I cannot help myself. I know not how
That moral force of which so much is spoken
   Will not sustain or fortify me now.
   I must, I must have help!

Some outside aid, some strength from spirit Sources,
   We all must have in hours like this, or die.
To one, or all of those mysterious Forces
   Which men call God, I lift my voice and cry,
   Come near, come near to me!

A SUGGESTION

As I go and shop, sir!
If a car I stop, sir!
   Where you chance to sit,
And you want to read, sir!
Never mind or heed, sir!
   I'll not care a bit.

For it's now aesthetic
To be quite athletic.

That's our fad, you know.
I can hold the strap, sir!
And keep off your lap, sir!
      As we jolting go.

If you read on blindly,
I shall take it kindly,
      All the car's not mine.
But, if you sit and stare, sir!
At my eyes and hair, sir!
      I must draw the line.

If the stare is meant, sir!
For a compliment, sir!
      As we jog through town,
Allow me to suggest, sir!
A woman oft looks best, sir!
      When she's sitting down.

A FISHERMAN'S BABY

Oh! hush little baby, thy Papa's at sea,
The big billows rock him as Mama rocks thee.
He hastes to his dear ones o'er breakers of foam.
Then hush little darling till Papa comes home.
Sleep little baby, hush little baby,
Papa is coming, no longer to roam.

The shells and the pebbles all day tossed about

Are lulled into sleep by the tide ebbing out.
The weary shore slumbers, stretched out in the sand,
While the waves hurry off at mid ocean's command.
Then hush little baby, sleep little darling,
Sleep baby, rocked by thy mother's own hand.

The winds that have rollicked all day in the west
Are soothed into sleep on the calm evening's breast.
The boats that were out with the wild sea at play
Are now rocked to sleep in the arms of the bay.
Then rest little baby, sleep little baby,
Papa will come at the break of the day.

CONTENT AND HAPPINESS

How is it that men pray their earthly lot
      May be 'content and happiness'? Dire foes
      Without one common trait which kinship shows
I hold these two. Contentment comes when sought,
While Happiness pursued was never caught.
      But, sudden, storms the heart with mighty throes
      Whenceforth, mild eyed Content affrighted goes,
To seek some calmer heart, less danger fraught.

Bold Happiness knows but one rival--Fear;
      Who follows ever on his footsteps, sent
      By jealous Fate who calls great joy a crime.
While in far ways 'mong leaves just turning sere,
With gaze serene and placid, walks Content.

No heart ere held these two guests at one time.

THE CUSINE

The woman who looks upon man as a sinner
Unsaved as to soul, and uncertain in heart,
Should learn how to cook, and prepare him a dinner,
And serve it with talent, refinement, and art.
Full many a question is solved by digestion.
Bad morals are caused, oftentimes by bad cooks,
And many a riot results from poor diet--
Conversion may lie in the leaves of cook books.

About the dull stalk of the thorntree of duty
Plant flowers of fragrance and vines of good taste.
Surround the coarse needs of the body with beauty,
Make common things noble, make vulgar things chaste.
Put art in housekeeping, nor think culture sleeping
Because the base animal, man, must be fed.
Delsarte should be able to speak in the table--
'Expression' may lie in a light loaf of bread.

Though hard be the labour, the end recompenses--
Though weary the journey, reward is the goal.
For the soul of a man must be reached through his senses,
As the senses of woman are reached through her soul.
Speak first to his spirit, he never will hear it;
Speak first to his body, his soul will reply;
The mortal man fare for, his appetites care for,

And lo! he will follow your footsteps on high.

Love born in the boudoir oft dies in the kitchen,
The failure of marriage oft starts in the soup.
The stomach appeal to, and men's heart you steal to--
Would you reach to the last? To the first you must stoop.

I WONDER WHY

Do you remember that glorious June
      When we were lovers, you and I?
Something there was in the robin's tune,
      Something there was in earth and sky,
That was never before, and never since then.
      I wonder why.

Do you remember the bridge we crossed,
      And lingered to see the ships go by,
With snowy sails to the free winds tossed?
      I never pass that bridge but I sigh
With a sense at my heart as of something lost.
      I wonder why.

Do you remember the song we sung,
      Under the beautiful starlit sky?
The world was bright, and our hearts were young--
      I cannot forget though I try and try.
How you smiled in my eyes while the echoes rung.
      I wonder why.

Do you remember how debonair
    The new moon shone when we said good-bye?
How it listened and smiled when we parted there?
    I shall hate the new moon until I die--
Hate it for ever, nor think it fair.
    I wonder why.

A WOMAN'S HAND

All day long there has haunted me
    A spectre out of my lost youth-land.
Because I happened last night to see
    A woman's beautiful snow-white hand.

Like part of a statue broken away,
    And carefully kept in a velvet case,
On the crimson rim of her box it lay;
    The folds of the curtain hid her face.

Years had drifted between us two,
    In another clime, in another land,
We had lived and parted, and yet I knew
    That cruelly beautiful perfect hand.

The ringless beauty of fingers fine,
    The sea-shell tint of their taper tips,
The sight of them stirred my blood like wine,
    Oh, to hold them again to my lips!

To feel their tender touch on my hair,
     Their mute caress, and their clinging hold;
Oh for the past that was green and fair,
     With a cloudless sky, and a sun of gold!

But the sun has set, and a dead delight
     Shadows my life with a dull despair,
Oh why did I see that hand of white,
     Like a marble ornament lying there?

PRESENTIMENT

As unseen spheres cast shadows on the Earth
     Some unknown cause depresses me to-night.
The house is full of laughter and sweet mirth,
     The day has held but pleasure and delight.

Down in the parlour some one blithely sings;
     A chime of laughter echoes in the hall;
But all unseen by other eyes, strange things
     Rat-like do seem to glide along the wall.

I rise, and laugh, and say I will not care;
     I call them idle fancies, one and all.
And yet, suspended by a single hair,
     The sword of Fate seems trembling soon to fall.

I leave the house, and walk the lighted street;

And mingle with the pleasure-seeking throng.
And close behind me follow spectre feet
    That pause with me, or with me move along.

I seek my room, and close and bolt the door;
    I draw the curtain, and turn up the light;
But close beside me, closer than before,
    This nameless ***something*** stands, but out of sight.

Ye mystic messenger of woe to come,
    Ye nameless nothing called 'Presentiment,'
Take form and face me; be no longer dumb,
    But tell who thou art, and wherefore sent.

TWO ROOMS

One room is full of luxury, and dim
    With that soft moonlit radiance of light
That she best loves, who sits and dreams of him
    Her heart has crowned as knight.

And one is bare, and comfortless, and dim
    With that strange, fitful glimmer that is shed
By candles casting shadows weird and grim,
    Above the sheeted dead.

In one, a round and beautiful young face
    Is full of wordless rapture; and so fair
You know her breast is joy's best dwelling-place;

You know sweet love is there.

In one, there lies a white and wasted face
    Whereon is frozen such supreme despair,
You need but look to know what left the trace;
    You know love **has been** there.

To one he comes! She leans her head of gold
    Upon his breast and bids him no more roam.
Ah God! Ah God! and one lies stark and cold,
    Because he ceased to come.

THREE AT THE OPERA

Last night the house was crowded. Were you there?
    You thought our box held only two, maybe--
Myself and chaperon, a matron fair.
    There was another whom you did not see.

Close, close beside me, sat a phantom form;
    Above the music and loud cheer on cheer
That rose, and thundered like a sudden storm,
    I heard his low voice whispering in my ear.

A dead man's voice. You know when dead men speak
    There is no noise their least tone will not drown.
His sweet soft words brought blushes to my cheek,
    And made my happy eyelids flutter down.

There were so many glasses turned on me,
     My chaperon was proud. She called me fair,
And said I drew their glances. Well, may be.
     I think they saw that dead man sitting there.

A dead man at an opera: how strange!
     I know it must have seemed much out of place.
He smiled, and spoke, and there was little change
     In the white pallor of his perfect face.

Yet he was dead. I knew it all the while,
     I do not wonder people looked that way.
It seemed so odd to see a dead man smile;
     Its strangeness never struck me till to-day.

He rose and went out when we left our stall;
     Rose up, went out, and vanished in the night.
He always sits beside me in that hall,
     But goes when goes the music and the light.

A STRAIN OF MUSIC

In through the open window
     To the chamber where I lay,
There came the beat of merry feet,
     From the dancers over the way.
And back on the wings of the music
     That rose on the midnight air,
My rare youth came and spoke my name,

And lo! I was young and fair.

Once more in the glitter of gaslight
     I stood in my life's glad prime:
And heart and feet in a rhythm sweet
     Were keeping the music's time.
Like a leaf in the breeze of summer
     I drifted down the hall,
On an arm that is cold with death and mould,
     And is hidden under the pall.

Once more at a low voice's whisper
     (A voice that is long since stilled)
I felt the flush of a rising blush,
     And my pulses leaped and thrilled.
Once more in a sea of faces,
     I only saw one face;
And life grew bright with a new delight,
     And sweet with a nameless grace.

A crash of passionate music,
     A hush and a silence then;
The dancers rest in their pleasure quest,
     And lo! I am old again.
Old and alone in my chamber,
     While the night wears wearily on,
And the pallid wraith of a broken faith--
     Keeps watch with me till the dawn.

SMOKE

Last summer, lazing by the sea,
    I met a most entrancing creature,
Her black eyes quite bewildered me--
    She had a Spanish cast of feature.

She often smoked a cigarette,
    And did it in the cutest fashion.
Before a week passed by she set
    My young heart in a raging passion.

I swore I loved her as my life,
    I gave her gems (don't tell my tailor).
She promised to become my wife,
    But whispered, 'Papa is my jailer.'

'We must be very sly, you see,
    For Papa will not list to reason.
You must not come to call on me
    Until he's gone from home a season.

'I'll send you word, now don't forget,
    Take this as pledge, I will remember.'
She gave me a perfumed cigarette,
    And turned and left me with September.

To-day she sent her 'cards' to me.
    'My presence asked' to see her marry
That millionaire old banker C---

She **has** my 'presents,' so I'll tarry.

And still I feel a keen regret
    (About the jewels that I gave her)
I've smoked the little cigarette--
    It had a most delicious flavour.

AN AUTUMN DAY

Leaden skies and a lonesome shadow
    Where summer has passed with her gorgeous train;
Snow on the mountain, and frost on the meadow--
    A white face pressed to the window pane;
A cold mist falling, a bleak wind calling,
    And oh! but life seems vain.

Rain is better than golden weather,
    When the heart is dulled with a dumb despair.
Dead leaves lie where they walked together,
    The hammock is gone, and the rustic chair.
Let bleak snows cover the whole world over--
    It will never again seem fair.

Time laughs lightly at youth's sad 'Never,'
    Summer shall come again, smiling once more,
High o'er the cold world the sun shines for ever,
    Hearts that seemed dead are alive at the core.
Oh, but the pain of it--oh, but the gain of it,
    After the shadows pass o'er.

WISHES

Whatever you want, if you wish for it long,
    With constant yearning and fervent desire,
If your wish soars upward on wings so strong
    That they never grow languid and never tire,--

Why, over the storm clouds and out of the dark
    It shall come flying some day to you.
As the dove with the olive branch flew to the ark,
    And the dream you have cherished--it shall come true.

But lest much rapture shall make you mad,
    Or too bright sunshine should strike you blind,
Along with your blessing a something sad
    Shall come like a shadow that follows behind.

Something unwelcome and unforeseen,
    Yet of your hope and your wish, a part,
Shall stand like a sentinel in between
    The perfect joy and the human heart.

I wished for a cloudless and golden day;
    It came, but I looked from my window to see
A giant shadow which seemed to say,
    'If you ask for the sunlight you must take me.'

Oh! a wonderful thing is the human will,

When seeking one purpose, and serving one end;
But I think it is wiser to just sit still,
    And accept whatever the gods may send.

THE PLAY

In the rosy light of my day's fair morning,
    Ere ever a storm cloud darkened the west,
Ere even a shadow of night gave warning
    When life seemed only a pleasure quest,
Why then all humour and comedy scorning--
    I liked high tragedy best.

I liked the challenge, the fierce fought duel,
    With a death or a parting in every act.
I liked the villain to be more cruel
    Than the basest villain could be in fact:
For it fed the fires of my mind with the fuel
    Of the things that my life lacked.

But as time passed on, and I met real sorrow,
    And she played at night on the stage--my heart,
I found I could not forget on the morrow
    The pain I had felt in her tragic part.
For alas! no longer I needed to borrow
    My grief from the actor's art.

And as life grows older, and therefore sadder
    (Though sweeter maybe with its autumn haze),

I find more pleasure in watching the gladder
    And lighter order of humorous plays.
Where the mirth is as mad, or maybe madder,
    Than the mirth of my lost days.

I like to be forced to laugh and be merry,
    Though the earth with sorrow and pain is rife:
I like for an evening at least to bury
    All thoughts of trouble, or pain, or strife.
In sooth, I like to be moved to the very
    Emotions I miss in life.

AS WE LOOK BACK (RONDEAU)

As we look back at our lost Used-to-Be,
'The light that never was on land or sea'
    Touches the distant mountain peaks with gold,
    And through the glass of memory we behold
Such blossoms as grow not on any lea.

The double leaf upon the poplar tree
Turns up its silver side to you and me,
And glow-worm lanterns light the lonely wold
    As we look back.

No sounds we hear but echoes of young glee;
No winds we feel but west winds blowing free,
    From those fair isles that seem a thousandfold
    More beautiful than in the days of old;

And all the clouds that hang above them flee,
    As we look back.

WHY

Why do eyes that were tender,
    Averted, turn away?
Why has our dear love's splendour
    All faded into gray?
Why is it that lips glow not
    That late were all aglow?
I know not, dear, I know not,
    I only know 'tis so.

Why do you no more tremble
    Now when I kiss your cheek?
Why do we both dissemble
    The thoughts we used to speak?
Why is it that words flow not
    That used to fondly flow?
I know not, dear, I know not,
    I only know 'tis so.

Have we outlived the passion
    That late lit earth and sky?
And is this but the fashion
    A fond love takes to die?
Is it, that we shall know not
    Again love's rapture glow?

I trust not, sweet, I trust not--
    And yet it may be so.

LISTEN

Whoever you are as you read this,
    Whatever your trouble or grief,
I want you to know and to heed this,
    The day draweth near with relief.

No sorrow, no woe, is unending;
    Though heaven seems voiceless and dumb,
Remember your cry is ascending,
    And an answer will certainly come.

Whatever temptation is near you,
    Whose eyes on this simple verse fall,
Remember good angels will hear you,
    And help you, so sure as you call.

Who stunned with despair, I beseech you,
    Whatever your losses, your need,
Believe when these printed words reach you--
    Believe you were born to succeed.

TOGETHER

We two in the fever, and fervour, and glow
   Of life's high tide have rejoiced together.
We have looked out over the glittering snow,
   And known we were dwelling in summer weather.
For the seasons are made by the heart, I hold,
   And not by the outdoor heat or cold.

We two in the shadows of pain and fear
   Have journeyed together in dim, dark places,
Where black-robed sorrow walked to and fro,
   And fear and trouble with phantom faces
Peered out upon us, and froze our blood,
   Though June's fair roses were all in bud.

We two have measured all depths, all heights;
   We have bathed in tears, we have sunned in laughter;
We have known all sorrow, and all delights,
   They never could keep us apart hereafter.
Wherever your spirit was sent I know,
   I would find my way in the dark, and go.

If they took my soul into Paradise,
   And told me I must be content without you,
I would weary them so with my homesick cries,
   And the ceaseless questions I asked about you,
They would open the gates and set me free,
   Or else they would find you and bring you to me.

ONE NIGHT

Was it last summer, or ages gone,
    That damp, dark night in the August dusk,
When I waited for you by the gate alone?
    And the air was heavy with scents like musk.
Swiftly and silently shooting down
    Like the lonesome light of a falling star,
I saw through the shadows dense and brown,
    The dull red light of your fine cigar.

Like a king who taketh his own, you came
    Through the lowering night and the falling dew.
Like one who yields to a rightful claim,
    I waited there in the dusk for you.
Never again when the day grows late,
    Never again in the years to be,
Shall I stand in the dark and dew, and wait,
    And never again will you come to me.

But always and ever when high and far
    The old moon hideth her troubled face,
I think how the light like a falling star
    Lit all my world with a new strange grace.
The passionate glow of your splendid eyes
    Shines into my heart as it shone that night,
And its slumberous billows surge and rise
    As the ocean is stirred by the tempest's might.

LOST NATION

Oh! we are a lone, lost nation,
     We, who sing your songs.
With his moods, and his desolation
     The poet nowhere belongs.

We are not of the people
     Who labour, believe, and doubt.
Like the bell that rings in the steeple,
     We are in the world, yet out.

In the rustic town, or the city
     We seek our place in vain;
And our hearts are starved for pity,
     And our souls are sick with pain.

Yes, the people are buying, selling,
     And the world is one great mart.
And woe for the thoughts that are dwelling
     Up in the poet's heart.

We know what the waves are saying
     As they roll up from the sea,
And the weird old wind is playing
     Our own sad melody.

We send forth a song to wander
     Like a spirit of ill or good;
And here it is heard, and yonder,

But is nowhere understood.

For the world it lives for fashion,
    For glory, and gain, and strife;
And what can it know of the passion
    And pain of a poet's life?

THE CAPTIVE

My lady is robed for the ball to-night,
    All in a shimmer and silken sheen.
She glides down the stairs like a thing of light,
    The ballroom's beautiful queen.

Priceless gems on her bosom glow--
    Half hid by laces a queen might wear.
Robed is she, as befits, you know,
    The wife of a millionaire.

Gliding along at her liege lord's side,
    Out-shining all in that company,
Into the mind of the old man's bride
    There creeps a curious simile.

She thinks how once in the Long Ago,
    A beautiful captive, all aflame
With jewels that weighed her down like woe,
    Close in the wake of her captor came.

All day long in that mocking plight,
     She followed him in a dumb despair;
And the people thought her a goodly sight,
     Decked in her jewels rare.

And now at her lawful master's side,
     With a pain in her heart, as great as then
(So thinks this old man's beautiful bride),
     Zenobia walks again.

NO SONG

These summer days when all the poets sing
     I have no voice for song.
I see the birds of summer taking wing,
     And days so sweet and long,
Each seemed a little heaven with no end,
I know are gone for evermore, dear friend.

Nay, by and by comes another Spring;
     And long, sweet, perfect days.
And by and by I shall have voice to sing
     My old glad, happy lays.
More blithesome songs, more days that have no end;
More golden summers; but **like thee** no friend.

TWO FRIENDS

One day Ambition, in his endless round,
All filled with vague and nameless longings, found
Slow wasting Genius, who from spot to spot
Went idly grazing, through the Realms of Thought.

Ambition cried, 'Come, wander forth with me;
I like thy face--but cannot stay with thee.'
'I will,' said Genius, 'for I needs must own
I'm getting dull by being much alone.'

'Your hands are cold--come, warm them at my fire,'
Ambition said. 'Now, what is thy desire?'
Quoth Genius, ''Neath the sod of yonder heather
Lie gems untold. Let's plough them out together.'

They bent like strong young oxen to the plough,
This done, Ambition questioned, 'Whither now?
We'll leave these gems for all the world to see!
New sports and pleasures wait for thee and me.'

Said Genius, 'Yonder ghostly ruin stands
A blot and blemish on surrounding lands;
Let's fling sweet, blooming fancies everywhere.'
Soon all the world in wonder came to stare.

'Come, come!' Ambition cried; 'Pray, do be gone
From this dull place: I would go further on.'
'There lies,' said Genius, 'up on yonder peak
A Prize, alone, I have not cared to seek.'

Up, up they went--as swift, as sure as Time,
They seemed to soar: (in truth they did but climb),
And there in sight of all the world beneath--
Ambition crowned fair Genius with a wreath.

All day they journeyed, swift from place to place;
Ambition led, and Genius joined the chase.
In every realm of fancy, or of thought,
All depths they sounded, and all heights they sought.

Now hand in hand for evermore they stray,
And if they part, or quarrel for a day,
You'll find Ambition, aimless, reckless, wild,
And Genius moping, like an idle child.

I DIDN'T THINK

If all the troubles in the world
      Were traced back to their start,
We'd find not one in ten begun
      From want of willing heart.
But there's a sly, woe-working elf
      Who lurks about youth's brink,
And sure dismay he brings alway--
      The elf, 'I didn't think.'

He seems so sorry when he's caught;
      His mien is all contrite;

He so regrets the woe he wrought,
    And wants to make things right.
But wishes do not heal a wound
    Or weld a broken link;
The heart aches on, the link is gone,
    All through--'I didn't think.'

I half believe that ugly sprite,
    Bold, wicked, 'I don't care,'
In life's long run less harm has done
    Because he is so rare;
And one can be so stern with him,
    Can make the monster shrink;
But, lack a day, what can we say
    To whining 'Didn't think'?

This most unpleasant imp of strife
    Pursues us everywhere.
There's scarcely one whole day of life
    He does not cause us care;
Small woes and great he brings the world,
    Strong ships are forced to sink,
And trains from iron track are hurled, alack,
    By stupid 'Didn't think.'

When brain is comrade to the heart,
    And heart from soul draws grace,
'I didn't think will quick depart
    For lack of resting-place.
If from that great, unselfish stream,
    The Golden Rule we drink,
We'll keep God's laws, and have no cause
    To say 'I didn't think.'

A BURIAL

To-day I had a burial of my dead.
　　　There was no shroud, no coffin, and no pall,
No prayers were uttered and no tears were shed--
　　　I only turned a picture to the wall.

A picture that had hung within my room
　　　For years and years; a relic of my youth.
It kept the rose of love in constant bloom
　　　To see those eyes of earnestness and truth.

At hours wherein no other dared intrude,
　　　I had drawn comfort from its smiling grace.
Silent companion of my solitude,
　　　My soul held sweet communion with that face.

I lived again the dream so bright, so brief,
　　　Though wakened as we all are by some Fate;
This picture gave me infinite relief,
　　　And did not leave me wholly desolate.

To-day I saw an item, quite by chance,
　　　That robbed me of my pitiful poor dole:
A marriage notice fell beneath my glance,
　　　And I became a lonely widowed soul.

With drooping eyes, and cheeks a burning flame,

I turned the picture to the blank wall's gloom.
My very heart had died in me of shame,
    If I had left it smiling in my room.

Another woman's husband. So, my friend,
    My comfort, my sole relic of the past,
I bury thee, and, lonely, seek the end.
    Swift age has swept my youth from me at last.

THEIR FACES

O Beautiful white Angels! who control
The inner workings of each poet soul,
Thou who hast touched my mind with tender graces
Come near to me that I may see thy faces.

Me, didst thou bless before I came to earth;
Me, hast thou kissed, and dowered at my birth,
With such a wealth of sweet imaginings,
That, even in sleep, my dreaming fancy sings.

Sometimes when seeing snow-white clouds at noon,
Or watching silver shadows from the moon,
Within my soul has stirred a joy like fear,
As if some kindred spirit lingered near.

Come closer, Angels! thou whose haloed wings
Do gild for me the meanest ways and things,
With beauty borrowed from the Infinite--

Stand forth, let me behold thee in the light.

O thought supreme! O death! O life! unknown
I shall not solve thy mystery alone.
The angels who have kissed me at my birth
Shall take again my soul when done with earth,
And as we soar through vast, star-lighted spaces,
At last, at last I shall behold their faces.

THE LULLABY

When the long day leans to the twilight,
     When the Evening star climbs to the moon,
With a heart that is silently breaking,
     I sit in the gloaming and croon.
I croon a low song for my darling,
     My wee one, my baby, my own;
Who, cradled in rosewood and velvet,
     Sleeps out in the churchyard alone.

Alone with no arms to enfold her,
     Alone with no pillowing breast,
Alone with no hand on her cradle,
     To rock her to soundlier rest.
But each day in the hush of the twilight,
     Is silenced my broken heart's cry;
And I sit where I sat with my darling,
     And sing her the old lullaby.

Oh! the dreams that come back to me mocking,
    The sorrow that makes the days long;
As I sit in the twilight there rocking,
    And singing that lullaby song.
But I think my wee darling rests better
    As the night shadows lengthen, and creep
Across her low bed, in the churchyard,
    If her mother's voice sings her to sleep.
And so with a heart that is breaking
    I sing the old 'Lullaby dear'
That hushed her so oft into slumber--
    O baby--my own--do you hear?

MIRAGE

When the beautiful mountain ash is turning--
    As lovely a sight as the eyes desire;
When the leaves of the sumac bush are burning,
    Like the steady flame of a winter fire;
When the weeds by the roadside all grow golden,
    When maples are glowing and asters gleam,
It is then that the new is changed to the olden,
    And back to my heart comes the past like a dream.

Like a mirage I see the blue haze o'er me,
    The City of Youth that I left behind.
Oh! whitely its turrets are gleaming before me,
    And out of the window lean faces kind.
And I hear the echo of jubilant voices;

There are cheeks of beauty and eyes of truth:
And every pulse in my heart rejoices--
There's no other place like the City of Youth.

And lo! the City is full of splendour,
And a voice in my soul breaks into song.
Yes, a passionate love, as fair as tender,
Creeps out of the grave where it slept so long.
As the strings of a harp by winds are shaken,
To endless music my heart is stirred,
When my name is breathed and my hand is taken,
Though I cannot utter a single word.

But with souls that are full of the beautiful weather,
And the perfect peace that has no name,
Under the autumn skies together
We stray, by the sumacs all aflame.
And the forest flushes to fuller glory:
Brighter glow asters and golden rod,
As eye unto eye tells the old, old story,
And the sunlight seems like the smile of God.

Alone I stand and sorrowful hearted;
The dead leaves fall in the chilly wind.
The mirage is fled, and the glory departed,
And the City of Youth is far behind.

ALONE IN THE HOUSE

I am all alone in the house to-night;
    They would not have gone away
Had they known of the terrible, bloodless fight
    I have held with my heart to-day.
With the old sweet love and the old fierce pain
    I have battled hour by hour;
But the fates have willed that the strife is vain.
Alone in the hour my thoughts have reign,
    And I yield myself to their power.

Yield myself to the old time charm
    Of a dream of vanished bliss,
The thrill of a voice, and the fold of an arm,
    And a red lip's lingering kiss.
It all comes back like a flowing tide;
    That brief, but beautiful day.
Though it oft is checked by the dam of pride,
Till the waters flow back to the other side,
    To-night it has broken away.

I gave you all that I had to give,
    O love, the lavish whole.
And you threw it away, and now I live
    A starved and beggared soul.
And I feed on crumbs that memory throws
    From her table over-filled,
And I lay awake when others repose,
And slake my thirst when no one knows,
    With the wine that she has spilled.

I go my way and I do my part
     In the world's great scene of strife,
But I do it all with an empty heart,
     Dead to the best of life.
And ofttimes weary and tempest tossed,
     When I am not ruled by pride,
I wish ere the die was throne and lost,
Ere I played for love without counting the cost,
     That I, like my heart, had died.

AN OLD BOUQUET

I opened a long closed drawer to-day,
And among the souvenirs stored away
Were the faded leaves of an old bouquet.

Those faded leaves were as white as snow,
With a background of green, to make them show,
When you gave them to me long years ago.

They carried me back in a flash of light
To a perfumed, perfect summer night,
And a rider who came on a steed of white.

I can see it all--how you rode down
Like a knight of old, from the dusty town,
With a passionate glow in your eyes of brown.

Again I stand by the garden gate,
While the golden sun slips low, and wait
And watch your coming, my love, my fate.

Young and handsome and debonair
You leap to my side in the garden there,
And I take your flowers, and call them fair.

Out of the west the glory dies,
As we stand under the sunset skies,
With love in our hearts, and love in our eyes.

Love too tender and love too great
To die with death, or to yield to fate;
But your restless steed tells the hour is late.

You mount him again and you ride away
Into the west that is growing gray.
Oh! turn the key on that dear bouquet.

It is dry and faded and I am old:
And the hand that gave it is green with mould,
And the winter of life is cold--so cold.

AT THE BRIDAL

Oh! but the bride was lovely,
      Oh! but the scene was bright,
And why was the bridegroom's face as pale

As his lady's robe of white?

Did you not see beside him
        A guest unasked, unbid?
Who came up the aisle with silent feet
        And gazed at him? he did!

He saw her eyes upon him,
        He felt her icy breath;
And under the bride's warm clinging hand
        There crept the touch of death.

And above the low responses
        There fell upon his ear
A voice forbidding the nuptial banns;
        But no one else could hear.

And when the ring was given,
        And when the prayer was said,
He knew, as he led his bride away,
        That he was not truly wed.

And while they sat at the banquet,
        And mirth flowed like the wine,
A dead girl's voice hissed in his ear,
        'You are not hers, but mine.'

Oh! never beside his hearthstone,
        And never in any place,
Shall he be free from the haunting thought
        Of that accusing face.

BEST

In the gruesome night and the wintry weather,
     I watched two dear friends die,
And I buried them both in one grave together.
     Oh! who is so sad as I?
For the old love, and the old year,
     They both have passed away;
And I never can find the old cheer
     Come what will or may.

I heard the bell in the tall church steeple
     Clang out a joyful strain.
And I thought, 'Of all the great world's people,
     I have the bitterest pain.'
For the old year was a good year,
     And the old love was sweet;
And how could my heart hold any cheer
     When both lay dead at my feet.

Life may smile and the skies may brighten,
     Winter will pass with its snows;
Grief will wane and the burden lighten--
     And June will come with the rose.
But it cannot bring the old cheer
     To fill my empty breast;
For the old year was the one year,
     And the old love was best.

The Codes Of Hammurabi And Moses
W. W. Davies

QTY

The discovery of the Hammurabi Code is one of the greatest achievements of archaeology, and is of paramount interest, not only to the student of the Bible, but also to all those interested in ancient history...

Religion   **ISBN:** *1-59462-338-4*   **Pages:132**
MSRP $12.95

The Theory of Moral Sentiments
Adam Smith

QTY

This work from 1749. contains original theories of conscience amd moral judgment and it is the foundation for systemof morals.

Philosophy **ISBN:** *1-59462-777-0*   **Pages:536**
MSRP $19.95

Jessica's First Prayer
Hesba Stretton

QTY

In a screened and secluded corner of one of the many railway-bridges which span the streets of London there could be seen a few years ago, from five o'clock every morning until half past eight, a tidily set-out coffee-stall, consisting of a trestle and board, upon which stood two large tin cans, with a small fire of charcoal burning under each so as to keep the coffee boiling during the early hours of the morning when the work-people were thronging into the city on their way to their daily toil...

Pages:84

Childrens   **ISBN:** *1-59462-373-2*   *MSRP $9.95*

My Life and Work
Henry Ford

QTY

Henry Ford revolutionized the world with his implementation of mass production for the Model T automobile. Gain valuable business insight into his life and work with his own auto-biography... "We have only started on our development of our country we have not as yet, with all our talk of wonderful progress, done more than scratch the surface. The progress has been wonderful enough but..."

Pages:300

Biographies/   **ISBN:** *1-59462-198-5*   *MSRP $21.95*

The Art of Cross-Examination
Francis Wellman

QTY

I presume it is the experience of every author, after his first book is published upon an important subject, to be almost overwhelmed with a wealth of ideas and illustrations which could readily have been included in his book, and which to his own mind, at least, seem to make a second edition inevitable. Such certainly was the case with me; and when the first edition had reached its sixth impression in five months, I rejoiced to learn that it seemed to my publishers that the book had met with a sufficiently favorable reception to justify a second and considerably enlarged edition. ...

Pages:412

Reference   **ISBN:** *1-59462-647-2*   *MSRP $19.95*

On the Duty of Civil Disobedience
Henry David Thoreau

QTY

Thoreau wrote his famous essay, On the Duty of Civil Disobedience, as a protest against an unjust but popular war and the immoral but popular institution of slave-owning. He did more than write—he declined to pay his taxes, and was hauled off to gaol in consequence. Who can say how much this refusal of his hastened the end of the war and of slavery ?

Law   **ISBN:** *1-59462-747-9*   **Pages:48**
MSRP $7.45

Dream Psychology Psychoanalysis for Beginners
Sigmund Freud

QTY

Sigmund Freud, born Sigismund Schlomo Freud (May 6, 1856 - September 23, 1939), was a Jewish-Austrian neurologist and psychiatrist who co-founded the psychoanalytic school of psychology. Freud is best known for his theories of the unconscious mind, especially involving the mechanism of repression; his redefinition of sexual desire as mobile and directed towards a wide variety of objects; and his therapeutic techniques, especially his understanding of transference in the therapeutic relationship and the presumed value of dreams as sources of insight into unconscious desires.

Pages:196

Psychology   **ISBN:** *1-59462-905-6*   *MSRP $15.45*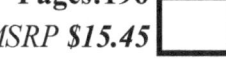

The Miracle of Right Thought
Orison Swett Marden

QTY

Believe with all of your heart that you will do what you were made to do. When the mind has once formed the habit of holding cheerful, happy, prosperous pictures, it will not be easy to form the opposite habit. It does not matter how improbable or how far away this realization may see, or how dark the prospects may be, if we visualize them as best we can, as vividly as possible, hold tenaciously to them and vigorously struggle to attain them, they will gradually become actualized, realized in the life. But a desire, a longing without endeavor, a yearning abandoned or held indifferently will vanish without realization.

Pages:360

Self Help   **ISBN:** *1-59462-644-8*   *MSRP $25.45*

QTY

The Rosicrucian Cosmo-Conception Mystic Christianity *by Max Heindel*　ISBN: *1-59462-188-8*　**$38.95**
The Rosicrucian Cosmo-conception is not dogmatic, neither does it appeal to any other authority than the reason of the student. It is: not controversial, but is: sent forth in the, hope that it may help to clear...　New Age/Religion Pages 646

Abandonment To Divine Providence *by Jean-Pierre de Caussade*　ISBN: *1-59462-228-0*　**$25.95**
"The Rev. Jean Pierre de Caussade was one of the most remarkable spiritual writers of the Society of Jesus in France in the 18th Century. His death took place at Toulouse in 1751. His works have gone through many editions and have been republished...　Inspirational/Religion Pages 400

Mental Chemistry *by Charles Haanel*　ISBN: *1-59462-192-6*　**$23.95**
Mental Chemistry allows the change of material conditions by combining and appropriately utilizing the power of the mind. Much like applied chemistry creates something new and unique out of careful combinations of chemicals the mastery of mental chemistry...　New Age Pages 354

The Letters of Robert Browning and Elizabeth Barret Barrett 1845-1846 vol II　ISBN: *1-59462-193-4*　**$35.95**
by Robert Browning and Elizabeth Barrett　Biographies Pages 596

Gleanings In Genesis (volume I) *by Arthur W. Pink*　ISBN: *1-59462-130-6*　**$27.45**
Appropriately has Genesis been termed "the seed plot of the Bible" for in it we have, in germ form, almost all of the great doctrines which are afterwards fully developed in the books of Scripture which follow...　Religion/Inspirational Pages 420

The Master Key *by L. W. de Laurence*　ISBN: *1-59462-001-6*　**$30.95**
In no branch of human knowledge has there been a more lively increase of the spirit of research during the past few years than in the study of Psychology, Concentration and Mental Discipline. The requests for authentic lessons in Thought Control, Mental Discipline and...　New Age/Business Pages 422

The Lesser Key Of Solomon Goetia *by L. W. de Laurence*　ISBN: *1-59462-092-X*　**$9.95**
This translation of the first book of the "Lemegton" which is now for the first time made accessible to students of Talismanic Magic was done, after careful collation and edition, from numerous Ancient Manuscripts in Hebrew, Latin, and French...　New Age/Occult Pages 92

Rubaiyat Of Omar Khayyam *by Edward Fitzgerald*　ISBN:*1-59462-332-5*　**$13.95**
Edward Fitzgerald, whom the world has already learned, in spite of his own efforts to remain within the shadow of anonymity, to look upon as one of the rarest poets of the century, was born at Bredfield, in Suffolk, on the 31st of March, 1809. He was the third son of John Purcell...　Music Pages 172

Ancient Law *by Henry Maine*　ISBN: *1-59462-128-4*　**$29.95**
The chief object of the following pages is to indicate some of the earliest ideas of mankind, as they are reflected in Ancient Law, and to point out the relation of those ideas to modern thought.　Religion/History Pages 452

Far-Away Stories *by William J. Locke*　ISBN: *1-59462-129-2*　**$19.45**
"Good wine needs no bush, but a collection of mixed vintages does. And this book is just such a collection. Some of the stories I do not want to remain buried for ever in the museum files of dead magazine-numbers an author's not unpardonable vanity..."　Fiction Pages 272

Life of David Crockett *by David Crockett*　ISBN: *1-59462-250-7*　**$27.45**
"Colonel David Crockett was one of the most remarkable men of the times in which he lived. Born in humble life, but gifted with a strong will, an indomitable courage, and unremitting perseverance...　Biographies/New Age Pages 424

Lip-Reading *by Edward Nitchie*　ISBN: *1-59462-206-X*　**$25.95**
Edward B. Nitchie, founder of the New York School for the Hard of Hearing, now the Nitchie School of Lip-Reading, Inc, wrote "LIP-READING Principles and Practice". The development and perfecting of this meritorious work on lip-reading was an undertaking...　How-to Pages 400

A Handbook of Suggestive Therapeutics, Applied Hypnotism, Psychic Science　ISBN: *1-59462-214-0*　**$24.95**
by Henry Munro　Health/New Age/Health/Self-help Pages 376

A Doll's House: and Two Other Plays *by Henrik Ibsen*　ISBN: *1-59462-112-8*　**$19.95**
Henrik Ibsen created this classic when in revolutionary 1848 Rome. Introducing some striking concepts in playwriting for the realist genre, this play has been studied the world over.　Fiction/Classics/Plays 308

The Light of Asia *by sir Edwin Arnold*　ISBN: *1-59462-204-3*　**$13.95**
In this poetic masterpiece, Edwin Arnold describes the life and teachings of Buddha. The man who was to become known as Buddha to the world was born as Prince Gautama of India but he rejected the worldly riches and abandoned the reigns of power when...　Religion/History/Biographies Pages 170

The Complete Works of Guy de Maupassant *by Guy de Maupassant*　ISBN: *1-59462-157-8*　**$16.95**
"For days and days, nights and nights, I had dreamed of that first kiss which was to consecrate our engagement, and I knew not on what spot I should put my lips..."　Fiction/Classics Pages 240

The Art of Cross-Examination *by Francis L. Wellman*　ISBN: *1-59462-309-0*　**$26.95**
Written by a renowned trial lawyer, Wellman imparts his experience and uses case studies to explain how to use psychology to extract desired information through questioning.　How-to/Science/Reference Pages 408

Answered or Unanswered? *by Louisa Vaughan*　ISBN: *1-59462-248-5*　**$10.95**
Miracles of Faith in China　Religion Pages 112

The Edinburgh Lectures on Mental Science (1909) *by Thomas*　ISBN: *1-59462-008-3*　**$11.95**
This book contains the substance of a course of lectures recently given by the writer in the Queen Street Hail, Edinburgh. Its purpose is to indicate the Natural Principles governing the relation between Mental Action and Material Conditions...　New Age/Psychology Pages 148

Ayesha *by H. Rider Haggard*　ISBN: *1-59462-301-5*　**$24.95**
Verily and indeed it is the unexpected that happens! Probably if there was one person upon the earth from whom the Editor of this, and of a certain previous history, did not expect to hear again...　Classics Pages 380

Ayala's Angel *by Anthony Trollope*　ISBN: *1-59462-352-X*　**$29.95**
The two girls were both pretty, but Lucy who was twenty-one who supposed to be simple and comparatively unattractive, whereas Ayala was credited, as her Bombwhat romantic name might show, with poetic charm and a taste for romance. Ayala when her father died was nineteen...　Fiction Pages 484

The American Commonwealth *by James Bryce*　ISBN: *1-59462-286-8*　**$34.45**
An interpretation of American democratic political theory. It examines political mechanics and society from the perspective of Scotsman James Bryce　Politics Pages 572

Stories of the Pilgrims *by Margaret P. Pumphrey*　ISBN: *1-59462-116-0*　**$17.95**
This book explores pilgrims religious oppression in England as well as their escape to Holland and eventual crossing to America on the Mayflower, and their early days in New England...　History Pages 268

QTY

The Fasting Cure *by Sinclair Upton*   ISBN: *1-59462-222-1*   **$13.95**
In the Cosmopolitan Magazine for May, 1910, and in the Contemporary Review (London) for April, 1910, I published an article dealing with my experiences in fasting. I have written a great many magazine articles, but never one which attracted so much attention...   New Age/Self Help/Health Pages 164

Hebrew Astrology *by Sepharial*   ISBN: *1-59462-308-2*   **$13.45**
In these days of advanced thinking it is a matter of common observation that we have left many of the old landmarks behind and that we are now pressing forward to greater heights and to a wider horizon than that which represented the mind-content of our progenitors...   Astrology Pages 144

Thought Vibration or The Law of Attraction in the Thought World   ISBN: *1-59462-127-6*   **$12.95**
by William Walker Atkinson   Psychology/Religion Pages 144

Optimism *by Helen Keller*   ISBN: *1-59462-108-X*   **$15.95**
Helen Keller was blind, deaf, and mute since 19 months old, yet famously learned how to overcome these handicaps, communicate with the world, and spread her lectures promoting optimism. An inspiring read for everyone...   Biographies/Inspirational Pages 84

Sara Crewe *by Frances Burnett*   ISBN: *1-59462-360-0*   **$9.45**
In the first place, Miss Minchin lived in London. Her home was a large, dull, tall one, in a large, dull square, where all the houses were alike, and all the sparrows were alike, and where all the door-knockers made the same heavy sound...   Childrens/Classic Pages 88

The Autobiography of Benjamin Franklin *by Benjamin Franklin*   ISBN: *1-59462-135-7*   **$24.95**
The Autobiography of Benjamin Franklin has probably been more extensively read than any other American historical work, and no other book of its kind has had such ups and downs of fortune. Franklin lived for many years in England, where he was agent...   Biographies/History Pages 332

Name	
Email	
Telephone	
Address	
City, State ZIP	

☐ **Credit Card**   ☐ **Check / Money Order**

Credit Card Number	
Expiration Date	
Signature	

Please Mail to: Book Jungle
                 PO Box 2226
                 Champaign, IL 61825
or Fax to: 630-214-0564